That was one of Mandy's mama's commandments,
along with never stepping out in torn underwear,
never kissing a boy on the first date and never
wearing white shoes before Memorial Day.

As Mandy thought of Jack taking a shower just on
the other side of the door, she wondered whether
her mama was right—at least about the motel rooms.

She turned in time to see Jack step into the room.
The towel around his neck did nothing to hide the
contours of his torso, the slick skin tapering down to
his low-slung jeans. Mandy lowered her eyes, but her
attention lingered on the faded blue denim around
his fly.

"A man don't have to be no rocket scientist to figure
out where you two are headed," her brother had
said. For the first time, he'd been right.

ABOUT THE AUTHOR

With over twenty-five American Romance novels to her credit, Judith Arnold is one of the series's premier authors. Her versatility and uncanny ability to make us laugh and cry have become her hallmarks. Judith, her husband and two young sons make their home in Massachusetts.

Books by Judith Arnold

HARLEQUIN AMERICAN ROMANCE
304—TURNING TABLES
330—SURVIVORS
342—LUCKY PENNY
362—CHANGE OF LIFE
378—ONE GOOD TURN
389—A > LOVERBOY
405—SAFE HARBOR
449—OPPOSING CAMPS
467—SWEET LIGHT
482—JUST LIKE ROMEO AND JULIET

HARLEQUIN SUPERROMANCE
460—RAISING THE STAKES
509—THE WOMAN DOWNSTAIRS

Don't miss any of our special offers. Write to us at the following address for information on our newest releases.

Harlequin Reader Service
P.O. Box 1397, Buffalo, NY 14240
Canadian address: P.O. Box 603,
Fort Erie, Ont. L2A 5X3

JUDITH ARNOLD

OH, YOU BEAUTIFUL DOLL

Harlequin Books

TORONTO • NEW YORK • LONDON
AMSTERDAM • PARIS • SYDNEY • HAMBURG
STOCKHOLM • ATHENS • TOKYO • MILAN
MADRID • WARSAW • BUDAPEST • AUCKLAND

Published July 1993

ISBN 0-373-16496-3

OH, YOU BEAUTIFUL DOLL

Chapter One

There weren't too many people Jack Slater would do this for.

He wasn't a happy driver. Coming of age in Manhattan, he'd devised a theory: Driving either made a person homicidal or suicidal—or both.

But he wasn't in Manhattan now. He was on a twisty, loopy roller coaster of a road, not quite two lanes wide, winding through the backwoods border country of eastern Kentucky—searching for a mountain dweller with the hick name of Mandy Harlon, so he could get a doll.

The car he'd rented up in Huntington, West Virginia, wasn't designed for mountain roads. And it didn't help that a thin, steady drizzle was sifting through the dense foliage of the forest and coating the crumbling asphalt with a slick wet glaze.

Only for Moe, he muttered under his breath. Only for Moe Kaplan would he make this ridiculous trip to the middle of nowhere.

Up ahead he spotted the mouth of an unpaved driveway. On a rough-hewn post beside it a rustic aluminum mailbox read Harlon, painted in black letters so small he had to brake to a near halt to read them.

The clerk at the café down in the village had given him the right directions, after all. What with the guy's thick Appalachian accent, Jack hadn't understood half of what he'd said. "The Harlon place?" he had drawled. "Y'all rully wanna go up thayer? Coz it's a long drahv on a wahl road and if Mandy ain't 'spectin' you, she mot jes' slam the doh in ya face."

Jack had survived the long drive on the wild road, and he was counting on Mandy Harlon not to slam the door in his face. All he wanted was Moe's doll.

When he'd ordered it, the manager at the boutique on Madison Avenue had assured him that a custom-made model would take about four weeks. Twelve weeks later, here he was searching for the doll maker to pick up Moe's doll in person. Tonight he'd be on a plane back to New York and tomorrow morning, Moe would have the thing in his arthritic old hands.

The Harlon house looked like something out of L.B.J.'s War on Poverty. A sagging porch ran the width of the place in front, a frayed sofa to the left of the screen door, a broom propped up against the peeling clapboards to the right. The front yard was an uneven clearing of dandelions and crabgrass surrounded by the dense evergreen forest. An old pickup was parked on the dirt driveway, next to a chimney constructed of ugly gray concrete blocks that rose only a couple of inches above the tar-shingled roof. A tub of gardenias struggled valiantly to bloom at the foot of the listing wooden steps that led up to the porch.

The only thing out of character was the sound: not the faint taps of raindrops but the loud beat of music through the screen door.

Jazz. New York-style fifties bebop; a saxophone hopping all over the scale.

Seeing no doorbell, Jack rapped his knuckles against the screen door. The music was loud enough to drown out his knock.

He tried the knob. The screen door swung open, one more bit of proof that he was out of the city. People actually left their doors unlocked here.

He stepped into the small front parlor. It was furnished with pieces that chic folks would consider antiques but looked to Jack like leftovers from a rummage sale. An inner door led into another room, but Jack felt enough like a trespasser without proceeding through it.

"Hello?" he bellowed.

The music stopped. "Jessie?" A woman's voice reached him from deep within the house. "Is that you?"

"Uh . . . no," he called back.

A minute passed, and then a woman appeared at the inner door. She was young and slim, with a wild tumble of hair the color of fire, and eyes as blue as the sky, and skin as smooth and pale as Lenox china. Her white T-shirt draped loosely over her body, hinting at the taut round curve of her breasts, and her blue jeans showed off her long, sleek legs. She was barefoot, her toenails polished scarlet. Her lips were pursed—in surprise at the invasion of a strange man, no doubt, although the sweet pink shape of them seemed to invite a kiss.

Simply looking at her made his blood grow warm and his mind conjure up all sorts of intriguing, ridiculously inappropriate notions. He found himself wishing he were Jessie, whoever the hell he was, just to have this gorgeous woman welcoming him into the house.

He hid his feelings behind an impassive smile. "The name's Jack Slater. I'm looking for Mandy Harlon."

She eyed him up and down, her face shadowed by a slight frown. "You're looking *at* Mandy Harlon," she drawled.

So much for the wizened old country woman he'd pictured. There was no gingham dress and faded apron, no gray braids wrapped around her head, no corncob pipe protruding from her lips. No, this woman was nothing but young and nubile and . . .

Damn. She was incredible looking.

"What do you want?" she asked.

He considered his response. What he wanted at that moment he had no right wanting. He would be gone soon, returning to New York, mission accomplished. No sense getting sidetracked just because the doll maker happened to be a doll herself.

"I want Moe Kaplan's doll," he said.

"Huh?"

"I ordered a custom doll for Moe Kaplan. One of those dolls with the rose-quartz crystals inside them that are supposed to make your dreams come true."

A thin smile stretched her lips. Her eyes remained steady on him, giving nothing away. Nothing but shimmering blue light. "Uh-huh," she said, almost a purr.

He ignored the effect her eyes were having on him, and plowed ahead. "I ordered the doll almost four months ago at a boutique called Dido, in New York City. It should have been delivered back in February, and now it's the middle of April. The manager at Dido told me if I was tired of waiting, I could contact you myself."

She continued to regard him, her expression inscrutable. He hoped her next statement would extend beyond guttural murmurs. He wanted to hear that sultry, drawling voice of hers again.

"I don't suppose," she said, her gaze as cool and dry as the air was warm and damp, "it occurred to you to phone me."

"It did occur to me. You were unlisted."

"If Dido's passing around my address, I'm surprised they didn't just put my number up on a billboard while they were at it."

She sounded thoroughly annoyed. On the other hand, the way she called the boutique "Dah-do" sent a ripple of . . . *something* through him. Pleasure, heat, arousal—whatever it was, he liked it.

"Don't be mad at the store," he said. "They didn't want to give out your address, either."

"But they gave it to you."

He shrugged. When he wanted something badly enough, he usually figured out a way to get it. "Actually, all they gave me was Harrow, Kentucky. A guy down at the Sunnyside Café told me where you lived."

"Sounds like you went to quite a mess of trouble," she concluded, her eyes still cool, her lids at half-mast. "You really must want this doll."

"Moe Kaplan really wants it. Is it finished yet?"

She leaned against the doorframe and crossed her arms. Her stance drew his attention to her shoulders. They were wide for a woman's, but bony in a delicate way. Her throat was slender, and that hair, all fiery red, like lava spilling down her back....

Get the doll and go, he commanded himself. "I'll pay you directly," he offered. "I'll pay you a premium. Just finish up the doll for me, okay?"

"Why should I give it to you?"

He sensed the challenge in her velvety tone, in the tilt of her chin. "Why shouldn't you? I just said I'm going to pay you."

"You also said your name was Jack Slater. The doll is for someone named Moe Kaplan."

"I ordered it for him. Check the order slip. My name's on it."

She studied him. How many times, he wondered, did she have to look him up and down before she decided to believe him? He thought he looked pretty trustworthy. He'd gotten a haircut just last week, and he was wearing new jeans, a clean white shirt and a wool blazer for warmth. Did she want to see some ID, for God's sake?

Apparently not. She reached some inner conclusion about him—grudgingly. "I'm just finishing up some orders for Dido. I reckon Moe Kaplan's doll is one of them." She turned and strolled through the door, shifting her shoulders in a way Jack chose to take as an invitation to follow her.

They walked down a short hall into a kitchen large enough to serve as a workroom—and a music room, as well. Two huge speakers stood in the far corners of the room, and stereo components were arranged on wall shelves. One half of the room featured old kitchen fixtures, including a deep-basin sink and a cooking range connected to the concrete chimney by a quaint aluminum stovepipe. Storage bins, bolts of cloth, a wide workbench and a sewing machine occupied the other half.

Jack strode to the workbench. Several cloth dolls lay across it, flat except for their sculpted foam-filled heads. According to Moe, the dolls' bodies were stuffed with rose-quartz crystals, which allegedly gave the dolls the ability to make wishes come true. While offering no guarantees, the manager at Dido had sworn that many of her customers were convinced of the dolls' powers, and that at a cost of fifty bucks— triple that for a custom-made doll—they were worth the hope they offered.

Moe had already tried copper bracelets, mega-vitamins, daily doses of an acrid-smelling Chinese herbal concoction, and assorted prescriptions from the best doctors his abundant wealth could buy. But still his fingers were gnarled and swollen, his joints stiff and painful.

At seventy, Moe Kaplan was still addicted to his three handball games a week at the club. His arthritis was slowing him down, and he was willing to try any-thing—even a doll full of rose-quartz crystals—to re-lieve the pain and stiffness in his hands.

Of course he'd wanted a custom-designed model. So Jack supplied the shop with two photographs of Moe.

Mandy Harlon had put those photographs to good use. It took Jack no time to pick out the Moe Kaplan model among the lifeless cloth bodies on the table.

"This is great!" he said, genuinely impressed. Moe's dense eyebrows that refused to go gray to match the thick silver hair on his head, his triangular nose and chin, the impeccable pin-striped wool suit and the little black loafers at the ends of the doll's limp legs— the doll's resemblance to Moe was uncanny. "If you'll just stuff this thing, I can be on my way."

Mandy turned off the CD player and removed the disc. "You're an impatient man, Mr. Slater."

For a moment he was distracted by the motions of her hands. Her fingers were long and graceful; they looked practically boneless. "I have a right to be im-patient," he said, exerting himself not to think about those fingers, about the soft, smooth skin of her hands, about the way they'd feel on his body. "This thing was supposed to be finished months ago, and I've been waiting and waiting—"

"I've been waiting and waiting for my rose quartz shipment. It finally just arrived today. All my orders are backed up. People are waiting and waiting for these dolls, too." She gestured toward the other nearly finished dolls on the workbench.

"Then you ought to find a new supplier," he advised.

"He is a new supplier." Mandy circled the workbench and hauled a carton up from the floor. Jack hurried over to help her with it, but she shot him a withering look and carried the box to the table herself. "My old supplier was more dependable, but he took sick. I had to find a new one. And let me tell you, Mr. Slater, rose-quartz crystals don't come easy."

"If they did, you wouldn't be charging fifty dollars and up for a doll."

"Given what my time and labor are worth, I sure as hell would be."

The blunt confidence of her words took him aback. For a redheaded slip of a hillbilly, she was apparently a savvy businesswoman. Obviously gifted, and shrewd enough to distribute her wares through trendy New York boutiques. She might have a backwoods address and a backwoods accent, but he would be wise not to underestimate her.

Especially given her ability to jolt his hormones with a mere smile, with a toss of her blazing hair and a flutter of her hands.

She cut the carton open and withdrew a drawstring sack. A frown of puzzlement crossed her face; then she shrugged, picked up the Moe Kaplan doll, flipped it over, poked her fingers into the slit at the neck to hold it wide, and poured in the quartz pebbles, some clear and some pink hued, small and glinting as they caught light from the overhead fixture.

Jack watched as the doll's legs filled and grew stiff. Then its abdomen began to take shape, and then its arms. Mandy shook the doll around to distribute the tiny stones, added a few more, and tugged the sack's drawstring shut.

"You understand, Mr. Slater," she drawled, "that I'm doing you a big favor here."

Given that he was about to hand over a hundred and fifty dollars, she wasn't doing him any favor, big or small. "I'm your customer," he reminded her.

"So are they," she said, gesturing once more toward the lifeless dolls lying along the bench like the victims of some ghastly terrorist attack. "I'm doing you a favor by letting you cut to the head of the line. These orders are as late as yours." She studied him thoughtfully, as if not quite sure why she had granted him this privilege. Her eyes glittered more brightly than the quartz in her bag, and her lips curved again in an odd, perplexed smile.

"If the people who ordered these other dolls wanted to cut to the head of the line, they could have driven up that crazy mountain road like I did."

Mandy's smile changed, deepening with amusement and something more, something challenging, something so sexy it made his breath catch. "That road isn't crazy."

"Are you kidding? All those switchbacks, and no shoulders, and the blacktop crumbling.... If a car had been coming the other way, I would have been forced off the road."

"Maybe you're just a lousy driver."

He sensed the humor in her voice, in her feline smile, in her luminous eyes. She was teasing him. Being teased by a woman who looked like Mandy Harlon did dangerous things to his libido.

He busied himself retrieving his checkbook and a pen from the inner pocket of his blazer. "I'm as good a driver as I have to be," he retorted.

"I like that road," she said, settling into the chair by her sewing machine and switching on the built-in lamp. "It makes it harder for gentlemen like you to come 'round bothering me."

"If you'd delivered your dolls on time, I wouldn't have had to come around bothering you."

Mandy didn't respond. She merely stitched up the doll and hummed Dave Brubeck's "Take Five."

"You like fifties jazz," he said.

"Who said I like it?" she asked without looking at him.

He moved toward the sound system, curious about her collection of CDs. "You were playing Charlie Parker, and now you're humming Dave Brubeck."

"It helps me concentrate."

She didn't have many discs, but what she had indicated eclectic taste: jazz, rock, classic country and western, and Bach's B-minor Mass. A Kentucky mountain woman listening to Bach?

Turning from the shelf, he watched her work. He studied the way her hair spilled forward over her shoulders, exposing the nape of her neck. He saw the dainty protrusion of her spine where her head was bowed. It was the most tempting sight in the world.

Forget it. New York was a city of eight million people, over half of them female, many of them every bit as beautiful as Mandy Harlon—and a lot less feisty. He didn't need some rustic mountaineer with weird taste in music to stimulate his imagination.

And yet... and yet there was that vulnerable sliver of skin, half hidden by soft wisps of hair that lay against it like curling licks of flame. There was the line of her shoulders and the arch of her back, and those slender, agile fingers...

Jack opened his checkbook, suddenly anxious to leave. He didn't want to find Mandy Harlon attractive. He didn't want to be feeling the primal hunger she had unleashed inside him without even trying. He had a happy, healthy life in New York City; he didn't need to be getting hung up on a luscious redheaded stranger in Hicktown, Appalachia.

"You've gone to a lot of trouble, Mr. Slater," she said when she turned off the sewing machine. "It's just a doll, you know."

"If it's just a doll, why am I paying this much money for it?"

She grinned. "Because you believe in the quartz crystals?"

"I don't. Moe Kaplan does." Her tone perplexed him. He glanced up from his checkbook. "You don't believe in them, do you?"

"It doesn't matter what I believe." Her eyes were animated, but he couldn't decipher their message. Her smile was mysterious.

"Of course it matters what you believe."

She shook her head. "I just make the dolls, Mr. Slater. What people do with them after I make them is their own business."

"If you don't believe, why do you bother with the quartz crystals? Why don't you just stuff the dolls with gravel?"

"That would be cheating my customers. *They* believe. All I do is supply them with something they believe in. And you know, some folks say if you believe in something enough, it'll come true."

Listening to her talk in that wondrous, sultry drawl of hers, Jack could believe just about anything.

He had to get away from her, before she had him melting in a puddle at her feet. "Well," he said briskly. "I'm sorry I had to bother you at your home—"

"Next time, try patience, Mr. Slater."

He bristled. "Next time, get your orders done on time. I was patient for three months."

She shrugged. "Things happen. Sometimes you've just got to live with it."

No one knew that better than Jack. Plenty had happened in his thirty years of life, and he'd learned better than most how to live with it, and through it, and past it. He'd learned—without any help from a doll maker with enchanting eyes and an attitude. "Let me just write this check," he said briskly, "and then I'll be out of your hair."

"Make it out to Amanda Harlon, Incorporated."

Amanda. Just one throaty drawl from her and he lost his sense of self-preservation. He didn't want to be out of her hair. He wanted to be in it, deep, tangled in the thick coppery tresses.

He groped for an excuse to stay awhile longer. They could talk, and he could immerse himself in her sensuous hillbilly accent. Or they could remain silent, and he could immerse himself in her beauty.

He extended the check to her, and when she took it her fingertips brushed his palm. Her touch triggered a reaction throughout his nervous system.

"You can see yourself out, Mr. Slater."

Her chilly dismissal left frostbite on his soul. "Right," he muttered, tucking the Moe doll under his arm and stalking down the hall to the porch. He slogged across her weedy front yard, got into the car, and revved the engine a few times to let off steam.

Then he took a deep breath and ordered himself to calm down. He wasn't going to tackle the mountain road—and no matter what she said, it *was* a crazy road—until he was in complete control of himself.

So she was alluring. So he'd reacted more strongly than he'd expected. He had Moe's doll, he was headed for home, and he was sure to regain his equilibrium soon. Mandy Harlon would fade into his memory, and then fade from it, and he'd find plenty of other women to fill his fantasies and his life. New York women, not some descendant of the Hatfields and the McCoys.

He backed out of the driveway, flicked on the windshield wipers, and cruised slowly down the serpentine road. The doll lay on the seat next to him, its button eyes gaping at him.

No, he wouldn't spend another minute thinking about her. He'd gotten what he came for. End of story.

The rain was falling harder. A pair of headlights stabbed through the mist as a car approached from the opposite direction. Although it was only midafternoon, Jack decided to switch on his headlights. He braked and edged as far to the right as he could so the car could pass him.

A few minutes passed, and he noticed headlights again, this time bearing down on him from behind. As the car drew closer, he recognized it as the one that had passed him earlier. Maybe the driver was lost.

The car came closer yet, cruising fast, tailgating. He wished he could pull over and let the guy get in front of him, but the road was too narrow.

He accelerated as much as he dared. So did the car behind him.

Sighing, he tapped on the brakes a few times, then edged his right tires off the road. The car rolled up alongside him, but instead of passing, it stopped. A man seated in the passenger seat lowered his window, as if he wanted to talk to Jack.

Jack lowered his window, too—and found himself staring at the barrel of a revolver.

"Give me the doll," the man said.

Jack's heart began to pound. His vision came in and out of focus with each thumping beat. When his eyesight sharpened, he saw that the driver was also a man, that both he and the guy with the gun were about Jack's age, white, neatly put together. They looked vaguely familiar.

When Jack's eyesight blurred, all he saw was the gun.

"What?" he said, sounding absurdly calm.

"The doll," the man said, indicating the Moe doll with a wave of his gun. "Give it to me."

Sure, Jack thought. Sure, just hand over the doll. After all he'd been through.

Don't play games, a voice whispered inside him. *The man's got a gun. Just give him the damned doll.*

Another, much more stubborn voice whispered back, *Like hell.*

He rolled up his window, slammed his car into gear, swerved onto the asphalt ahead of the other car and flew down the mountain road, driving for his life.

Chapter Two

The crystals, she thought. Check the crystals.

She'd noticed something odd about them when she'd filled the doll Jack Slater had come for. But it had been hard to focus on anything besides him as long as he'd been in the house.

How strange that he'd traveled so far to get the doll in person. Customers simply didn't do that. If she'd wanted people showing up on her doorstep, she would have opened a store right here in Harrow.

True, her new quartz supplier, Albert Stevenson, had been late with this first shipment, but she was sure he'd be prompt next time. And the quality of the quartz he'd sent had seemed marvelous, more sparkly than usual. Maybe it contained more magic than the stuff her old supplier used to send.

She chuckled and shook her head. She herself had no faith in the mystical powers of quartz. But if that was what her customers wanted, that was what Mandy gave them.

She wanted to recheck the crystals to see if they were truly as sparkling as they'd seemed when she'd stuffed them into Jack Slater's doll. But thinking about Jack's doll made her think about Jack. What audacity, marching into her house as he had, following her into her kitchen, issuing orders . . . and gazing at her with such intense desire she could almost feel it wrapping around her like thick velvet, making her grow over-heated and restless.

Of course he hadn't desired her. All he'd desired was the doll. She was reading nonexistent ideas in the steady power of his dark eyes, the tousle of his hair, the thin, daring curve of his lips.

She was proud of how well she'd maintained her composure in his presence. The moment he'd left, though, she'd felt her spine go as limp as the un-stuffed dolls on the bench. Sinking into her chair, she forced herself to acknowledge the man's overwhelm-ing effect on her, the way her heart had jitterbugged whenever he stared at her with those deep-set brown eyes, the way she'd felt a smoldering warmth in the pit of her stomach whenever she inhaled his clean, woodsy scent. The way his hands had molded the air when he'd talked. The way his low, smoky voice with its edgy New York inflection had put her defenses to a test she wasn't sure they could pass.

He was a man of hard angles and aggressive lines, a man who entered a room and made it his own. Other people wandered in and out of her house without having such an impact. Folks visited, they talked, they asked favors or returned them—and then they departed, leaving Mandy in very much the same state she'd been in before they'd arrived.

Not Jack Slater.

She'd held her own with him, at least. He couldn't have guessed how much his eyes had mesmerized her and his long, lean body had transfixed her. Let him think she would finish a doll out of order for just any soul who happened along. No need for him to know she did it because that was her only chance to get rid of him. If he'd stayed in her house a moment longer...

She didn't know what might have happened. An explosion, maybe. A thunderstorm. She'd felt the air pressure plummeting, the atmosphere churning with electricity.

The crystals. Forget about Jack Slater from New York City and check the crystals.

She blinked a few times to erase his image from her mind, then went to the carton. She pulled out the top bag—one of several jammed into the carton. She was perplexed by the packing; Felix Crimmins used to send the quartz packed in a single large plastic bag inside a box. The cloth drawstring bags this new supplier used seemed awfully fancy for pebbles.

She spilled a handful of the crystals onto the bench. They weren't as pink as the rose quartz Felix used to send. Many of the stones were clear or silvery white, multifaceted, glittering as if illuminated from within.

She lifted one of the stones, held it up to the light and sucked in her breath.

"Oh, my God," she whispered, thinking about the stones she'd poured into Jack Slater's doll, the stones still in the bag, the dazzling stone in her hand.

It sure as hell wasn't quartz.

JACK WONDERED which was worse: death by bullet or death by car crash.

He gripped the wheel, steering the car this way and that, feeling the tires skid and slide on the rain-slick asphalt and dividing his attention between the road in front of him and the headlights behind him. He must be the world's biggest idiot, to have chosen to outrun these thugs.

But people didn't stick a gun in your face and demand a doll if the doll wasn't worth shooting you over. And if it was, he was going to hang on to it for as long as he still had a breath of life in him.

Who were those guys? Jack had known a few tough characters in his day, but never anyone such as this.

Friends of Moe's? Not likely. Moe had had little exposure to the seamy underbelly of society. In his heyday, he had mixed it up with corporate sharks, greedy bankers and wheeler-dealers, but not the sort of people who armed themselves with thirty-eight-caliber revolvers.

But those guys had looked familiar. Ordinary, really. The sort of guys he might have passed a thousand times on the crowded sidewalks of midtown Manhattan. Thirtysomething, dressed unobtrusively. Clean-shaven, nondescript, utterly unremarkable.

Except for the gun. Cripes. It was amazing Jack had been able to pick out any details at all with that gun aimed at the bridge of his nose.

The road swooped down and then rose precipitously. He accelerated into the ascent, and at the top the tires seemed to lose contact with the earth for an instant. He sped down the next slope. Behind him the headlights loomed larger.

They were gaining on him. His rental car could never outrun them. He was going to have to finesse them instead.

Ahead of him, the road forked. He switched off his headlights and took the left fork. They took the right, and he allowed himself a moment's satisfaction. Before he could get smug, he noticed the headlights looming in his mirror again.

Another fork. He turned right this time. The road banked, scaled a steep hill and sank sharply. Mist hovered above the ground, snagging in the ferns and brush to either side of him.

Branches lashed the sides of the car. Above him the sky was damp, gray, nasty. The headlights in the rearview mirror vanished, then reappeared, then vanished once more.

Through the murky fog, he spotted a dirt road veering off into the woods. He floored the gas pedal, hugged the asphalt as it bore right around the turn, and at the last minute swerved onto the dirt road.

His car bounced through the woods on the decrepit unpaved road. He heard sticks scratch against the fenders and door panels; he heard loose rocks rico-chet off the underside of the car.

If the road came to a dead end, he might come to a dead end, too.

A full, precious minute elapsed before he spotted the headlights behind him, way in the distance.

He drove faster, as fast as he dared. The dirt road zigged left and zagged right, between boulders, around trees. Mud splattered onto the windshield, and the wipers smeared it across the glass, smudging his vi-sion.

They were gaining on him again. He glanced down at the doll beside him, its stitched red mouth raised in a smile.

"I'm doing this for you, buster," Jack grunted, slamming on the brakes as the road skewed sharply to the left. "The least you could do is look worried."

The thugs were closing in, less than a hundred feet behind, less than fifty feet. The dirt road twisted, de-touring around an abandoned old barn, curving to the right at a ravine. Jack could hear the other car's en-gine like the breath of a runner on the back of his neck. Catching up. Catching up.

He had to fluster them, had to force a mistake. He hit the brake pedal hard, then floored the gas, then braked again, hoping to throw them into a spin.

He heard them skidding behind him, splashing through the mud, their tires squealing. He sped and then braked again. He saw by the dizzying arcs of their headlights that they were barely in control of their vehicle.

He braked hard once more—and felt his own car begin to fishtail in the slippery mud, lose traction, lurch toward the edge of the dirt road. And then over and down. And down.

Oh, God, he thought, just before his car crashed against the bottom of the ravine in a cacophony of rattling metal and groaning springs.

An eternity passed before the car stopped shuddering. Stillness claimed the air, followed by the loud crack of a tree branch snapping. The thick branch rolled down the steep slope, finally coming to rest against the trunk of his car.

He took a deep breath, then twisted in his seat and peeked through the cracked rear window. Above him on the road, he saw his pursuers reverse direction and head back up the dirt road.

Jack didn't know if the two men were going to come back for him. But he wasn't going to stick around to find out.

Grabbing the doll, he ducked out of the car and forged deeper into the forest. He had no idea where he was or where he was going. All he knew was that he had to keep moving, keep running.

All he knew was that he had to stay alive—and he had to hang on to the doll.

WHEN SHE HEARD someone at her door this time, she pulled her shotgun out of the mudroom off the kitchen, loaded it, and waited.

She'd already heard a car whip past her house a couple of times, eastbound, westbound, going up the mountain and down. That was more traffic than this winding forest road usually got in a day.

Just one more bit of strangeness on this strange afternoon. Jack Slater, an alien car zooming back and forth . . . and the crystals. The alleged crystals.

The carton from Albert Stevenson was tucked away in a cabinet in the cellar. She'd sifted through every cloth bag inside the box; all except the top one had contained quartz pebbles. But that top bag, the one whose contents she'd used to stuff Jack Slater's doll . . .

Whenever she thought about it, a shiver ran down her spine.

She'd been contemplating her options ever since she'd made her discovery. She'd considered telephoning Stevenson, but decided not to. What would she tell him? What if he'd mailed her the wrong stuff on purpose? What if he was up to something illegal?

That led her to consider talking to Bill McIntyre, Harrow's sole police officer. But Bill wasn't exactly incorruptible, and Mandy wasn't about to hand over the bag to him. For the moment it was hers, and as long as it was hers she could control what happened to it.

She'd tried Jessie's number. He wasn't home. She'd tried Felix, her old supplier, who had been the one to recommend Albert Stevenson, but his wife had said he was resting and couldn't be disturbed.

She thought about Jack Slater, his trek all the way to Harrow from New York City, his insistence on getting his doll. Maybe he had something to do with the bag of stones. If only she could figure out what.

Now someone was at her door. She heard no knock, just the rattle of the latch giving way as the person entered.

Mandy held her breath, lifted the shotgun to her shoulder, released the lock and braced the barrel with her left hand.

"Ms. Harlon..." The voice was muted, barely a whisper. She couldn't even tell if it belonged to a man or a woman. "Mandy Harlon..." And then an uneven step.

She held her breath and flexed her right index finger against the trigger.

Another stumbling step, another, and then he was in the kitchen doorway. Soaking wet, spattered with dirt and clinging to the doll he'd paid for no more than two hours ago.

He stared at her. Raindrops ran in rivulets from his dark brown hair to his chin, to his soggy jacket and mud-caked jeans and leather sneakers. A thin, jagged line of blood marred one otherwise perfect cheek, and his lungs pumped in and out like a fireplace bellows.

"Oh, great," he muttered, swabbing the water from his chin. "Now *you're* going to shoot me."

"I might. I haven't decided yet," she said, focusing on the waterlogged but shockingly handsome Jack Slater through one squinted eye as she kept the shotgun aimed. "Don't you believe in knocking before you enter?"

"If you had a doorbell, I'd use it. I mean, really, just a simple little doorbell. It would make the world a better place."

He sounded mildly delirious. She continued to watch as he struggled to catch his breath, as he mopped his wet face with an equally wet hand, as he shoved the dank locks of hair off his brow and revealed another bleeding cut above his left eye. She continued to watch as his legs buckled and he slumped down onto the floor.

Either he was a good actor or he was seriously hurt. Taking no chances, she kept her finger on the trigger as she approached him. He leaned back against the wall, gazing up at her and breathing hard. His hands cradled the doll, which looked to be in a whole lot better shape than Jack.

"Don't shoot me," he requested, sounding uncannily composed. "I don't think I could handle it right now."

She almost laughed. If he weren't bleeding, if he weren't obviously clinging to his last shred of energy, she would have. "What happened to you?" she asked.

"You tell me."

"I haven't any idea."

He appeared skeptical, his eyes narrowing on her. "Let's just say you aren't my first gun of the day. I've already had someone else take aim at me."

"Around these parts, lots of folks are hunters. Guns aren't a big deal."

"The last person who pointed a gun at me wasn't a hunter. He had a revolver. People don't hunt with revolvers—unless they're hunting other people."

She wasn't sure what to make of that. She knew of no one in Harrow besides Bill McIntyre who owned a revolver. And why would Bill—or anyone else, for that matter—want to hunt Jack Slater?

That question had to have an answer, but she wasn't sure she could rely on Jack to tell her. As it was, he appeared to be regarding her with as much distrust as she felt toward him.

"So. You came upon a gunman?" she asked carefully.

"Two men, one gun. I tried to outrun them in my car, and I drove over a cliff."

"Dear God." At that moment, she believed him. In her heart, at least, she believed. She felt on the verge of tears. She wished she could run her hands over his body in search of broken bones, and summon an ambulance, and take care of this poor, traumatized man.

Her bout of sympathy startled her. She had to force herself to remember she wasn't yet ready to trust Jack Slater, a man who had coincidentally entered her life at the same time her new shipment of quartz had.

"This must be what they mean by Southern hospitality," he muttered, his gaze straying back to her gun. "Would you mind putting that damned rifle away?"

"It's a shotgun, not a rifle."

"I'm sure there's a world of difference."

"There is," she said. She would have enlightened him, but he didn't seem interested. He rested his head against the wall, staring at the ceiling for a moment, and shivered.

The small gesture of discomfort reminded Mandy of the calamity he'd just endured. Two men, a gun, a car chase that resulted in his driving over a cliff. She recalled the car she'd heard not long ago, racing up and down the road abutting her property, and wondered whether it had anything to do with the men who'd chased Jack. She didn't like the idea of armed strangers cruising around her mountain, threatening people, hurting them.

She swallowed to smother the quiver in her throat. "Were these two men with the gun trying to rob you or just scare you?"

"They wanted my doll."

She nodded slightly. Whoever they were, they must have known what was inside the doll. "Why do you suppose they wanted it?" she asked with deceptive blandness, anxious to find out if Jack knew.

He sighed and closed his eyes for a minute. "Maybe they ordered one of your dolls months ago, and they got sick of waiting for it."

He didn't know about the stones, then. Of course not. He wouldn't have known unless he'd cut open the doll and seen for himself.

Setting the shotgun aside—within reach—she knelt down beside him. She wanted to examine him for hidden injuries. He could have bruises, broken ribs, pulled muscles. There was no way to find out without touching him, easing off his jacket, unbuttoning his shirt....

Merely thinking about it made her breath lodge in her throat. "How bad are you hurt?" she asked, appalled by the tremor in her voice.

"I'm not hurt at all," he said. "I'm just tired. I've been hiking through the forest for miles. I was looking for the Sunnyside Café, but I guess I took a wrong turn somewhere and wound up here instead."

"Your car went over a cliff. How could you not be hurt?"

"It was a little cliff."

"And you're bleeding."

"I am?"

She stood and went to the sink, where she dampened a clean dish towel with water. The scratches on his face had already been washed by the rain, and they didn't appear deep. But he winced when she touched the towel to his cheek, and again when she showed him the traces of blood on it.

"Tree branches, probably," he said.

"Let me get some bandages—"

"Leave it. I'm not going to die—unless one of the numerous people pointing guns at me sneezes while their finger's on the trigger."

"Jack..." She pressed the towel to his forehead, dabbing gently at the cut there. He gritted his teeth; she saw the pulse below his temple twitch. "I should take you to the doctor."

"You've got a doctor here in the sticks?"

She smiled wryly. "Yes, we've got a doctor. He lives only ten miles away, in the next holler."

"Holler?"

"Hollow," she enunciated. "That's what we call a valley here in the sticks."

He smiled grimly and shook his head. "Forget it. I just want to return to Huntington, straighten things out with the car-rental place at the airport and fly home."

"With the doll?" she asked.

He scowled. "Of course with the doll. If I didn't want the doll, I would have handed it over to that jerk with the gun."

She couldn't let him leave with the doll, not without first telling him what was inside it. Once he knew that, he would understand why someone had wanted to steal it from him. Someone who knew what was inside. Someone apparently willing to kill him for it.

She couldn't send Jack off in ignorance.

Yet to tell the truth, she had to trust him. Completely. Unwaveringly.

She gazed at him, thoughtful, assessing every nuance in his expression, his clenched jaw, his disheveled brown hair, his piercing eyes, his powerful hands. His apparent confusion. His straightforward words.

She took a deep breath, sent a silent prayer heavenward, and made her choice.

"I've got to show you something," she said, reaching for her gun.

He cursed. "If you're going to shoot me, don't show me."

"I'm not going to shoot you. It's just, we've got to go down to the cellar, and I'd like some protection with me."

"You know, if you were really interested in protection, you might try locking your front door."

"The lock's broken," she told him. "Jessie promised to fix it, but he's been busy. It hasn't been a problem till today."

Slowly, laboriously, Jack pulled himself to his feet. He wobbled, and she reflexively reached out to steady him. His hand clamped around her forearm, informing her that despite his weariness and his cuts, he was an astonishingly strong man. His grip was tight, his fingers thick, the skin of his palm hard and smooth.

She hoped she hadn't made a mistake trusting him. Because if she had, if he intended to hurt her, he wouldn't need a gun to do it.

Once he regained his balance, his hand relented on her, lingering for barely a moment before he let his arm drop. He glanced away, as if embarrassed that she'd seen him falter. Her arm tingled where he'd touched it, her skin warmer there than elsewhere. Her breath grew shallow at the thought of how those thick, hard fingers of his would feel on other parts of her body, and the thought embarrassed her far more than his bout of dizziness could have embarrassed him.

"Downstairs," she said with forced brightness, shoving open the door off the kitchen and flicking on the light switch.

She preceded Jack down the wooden steps, feeling them vibrate under his weight. The cellar was gloomy in spite of the naked bulb hanging from a cross beam at the center of the room. The stone floor radiated a chill, and the cabinets lining the walls shed spooky shadows across the room.

"It's over here," Mandy said.

Jack followed her to one of the cabinets and leaned against it as she pulled out the shipping carton from her supplier. She peered up at him before lifting the flaps. His gaze was not on the box but on her, his dark eyes surprisingly lucid, reflecting nothing of his ordeal over the past several hours.

She hoped she hadn't made a mistake in trusting him. If she had, he'd be as rich as sin, and she'd be dead.

Please, God, she prayed silently, let me be right about this man.

She lifted out a handful of stones for him to view.

His eyes widened and he called upon the Lord in a much cruder way than she had. "Is this what I think it is?'' he asked, lifting one particularly large crystal from her hand and scrutinizing it in the glaring light from the bulb.

"I'm not an expert. I can't say for sure."

"It's a diamond." He shot her a quick look as if expecting her to disagree.

She said nothing.

He reached into the sack and pulled out a handful of stones. His brow furrowed as he spread them across his palm, lifted one and studied it in the light, then put it down and lifted another. "They aren't all diamonds. This one definitely isn't."

"It's a mixture of diamonds and quartz."

He lifted another stone, squinted at it and shook his head. "You stuffed Moe's doll with diamonds?" he asked on a laugh.

"Not on purpose, believe me."

"Jeez." He laughed again and emptied his hand back into the sack. "I've already paid for the doll, so it's mine. If you've got a problem with that, have your lawyer call my lawyer."

"We both have a problem with that, Mr. Slater. You said those men wanted to kill you. Now I don't reckon it's my brilliant craftsmanship that makes them want your doll so much."

"You think they know it's stuffed with diamonds?"

"Why else would they want it?"

"How could they possibly know? You advertise that the dolls have rose-quartz crystals in them."

"That's what they're supposed to have in them. That's what I ordered. My supplier sent me mostly quartz, but this one sack..."

"Where was it shipped from?" Jack asked, turning to examine the carton. "The postmark says Brazil."

"I get my quartz from all over. I order it through the supplier in New York, and he imports it directly to me. That's the way my old supplier worked, and—"

Jack clamped his hand over her mouth and peered toward the stairs. Several seconds elapsed, and then she heard it, too: footsteps in the parlor above her, moving slowly, stealthily, toward the kitchen.

"In here," a man called out. "This must be where she makes the damned things."

"Honest to God," came another male voice, "why can't she work someplace normal? How many times did we drive past this shack?"

Overhead, Mandy heard them stalking through her kitchen, pushing her work bins around. She lowered her eyes to Jack's arm, arched around her shoulder. She felt the smoldering strength in it, the fierce power of his hold on her. She had to close her eyes, had to press her lips tightly shut to keep from tasting the hard skin of his palm.

"I told you we should have gone back to that diner in town and gotten directions," one of the men upstairs muttered. He didn't sound like a local; his accent was closer to Jack's gritty New York pronunciation.

"You can't go into a joint like the Sunnyside Café and ask the guy for the same directions twice. He'd get suspicious."

"Yeah, well, if you hadn't run that bozo off the road, he could have led us back here."

"Hey, come on, the guy's probably dead. Don't call him names. Show a little respect."

"He still has his doll."

"So what? I'm telling you, the odds of that doll having the stuff inside is zilch. I wish you'd let me handle everything. You scared him off, you went and killed him, and—"

"Nobody killed nobody. That guy's here."

"What do you mean?"

"He's got to be here somewhere. Look, there's his doll sitting on the floor over there."

"Damn," Jack whispered. "That's Moe's doll."

"Maybe that's a different doll," said one of the men in the kitchen.

"It looks like his doll."

"How could he have gotten here? He's dead."

"You know what they say. These dolls are supposed to bring good luck or something. Maybe the doll kept him alive."

"Take it. We'll check it later."

Jack struggled with the urge to race up the stairs. Reason got the better of him, and he nodded toward the bulkhead door leading out into the backyard. "Let's go," he mouthed, tucking the sack of diamonds into his blazer pocket.

Mandy resented his taking charge—to say nothing of his taking the diamonds. But she couldn't possibly jam the sack into a pocket of her snug-fitting jeans, and she couldn't think of a better idea than what he'd suggested. If the men had found Jack's doll, they were close to the inside door to the cellar. And they had a revolver.

"Light's on down here," one of them shouted from near the top of the stairs.

Jack released Mandy's mouth and grabbed her hand. Clinging to her shotgun, she ran across the room with him and tugged on the inner latch. The men's footsteps on the plank stairway echoed through the cellar.

"There!" one of them shouted as the bulkhead door swung open. "Over there!"

"Run," Jack ordered her, shoving her ahead of him up the cement steps.

The two men raced through the cellar toward the bulkhead steps. As soon as Jack was outside, Mandy spun around and aimed the shotgun. "Don't move," she warned the men.

They hesitated at the sight of the shotgun. "Hey, lady," the closer one cooed in an ameliorating voice. He scaled the next step, and the next, his hands raised palm out on either side of his face. "Let's not do anything hasty."

"What are you doing in my house?" she drawled.

The second one was reaching into his pocket. Jack sprang forward from behind her, hurtling himself at them and shoving them both backward down the stairs, into the cellar. Mandy slammed down one of the sloping bulkhead doors as Jack slammed down the other. He shoved a stick through the handles to secure the doors.

"They're going to come up through the kitchen," he said. "Let's get the hell out of here."

"Get in the truck." Mandy ran barefoot through to the driveway at the side of the house.

"You get in and start the engine." He darted past the truck to the thugs' car, which blocked the driveway. Mandy climbed into the truck and twisted the key, which she always left in the ignition.

The engine coughed to life. In the mirror she saw Jack hunkering down beside the car. Then she saw one of the men staggering out of the front door.

"Jack! Come on!" she hollered.

He glanced over his shoulder and he saw the man heading for him. With amazing agility, he sprang to his feet, leaped over the tailgate into the flatbed and shouted, "Go!"

She steered forward, bumping over the ruts and grass of her backyard, circling her house and emerging into the front yard. She steered carefully around the tub of gardenias and between two trees, coming up onto the driveway behind the car.

In her mirror she saw the man fire at the truck. She heard the bullet whistle through the air, then yanked on the steering wheel and sped onto the road, up the hill.

Her heart pounded wildly against her ribs. Her breath came in short gulps. In the flatbed she heard nothing. Was Jack shot?

She knew the men would have no trouble catching up to her if she stopped. But she had to see if Jack was all right. Shifting into neutral, she threw open her door and climbed out.

Jack slowly sat up. His clothes and hair were drenched with rain. He rolled his shoulders to loosen them. Noticing her standing beside the truck, watching him, he gave her a crooked smile.

"Are you all right?" Her voice fluctuated, fear and relief staging a battle somewhere in her throat.

"A little black and blue, but I'll live."

"They shot at you!"

"They missed." He slung one leg over the side of the truck, then the other. Without thinking, Mandy wrapped her arms around him and helped him down.

She wanted to hang on to him forever. He was alive, and it felt so good just to hold him, just to feel him warm and breathing in her arms. It felt so good to press against him, to take shelter in his embrace, to lean into his tall, taut body.

Then her wrist bumped against the bulky sack in his jacket pocket. The diamonds.

She drew back. As long as he and not she had the diamonds, her trust in him was a shaky thing. And as long as it felt so heavenly to embrace him, her trust in herself was just as shaky.

"Better get inside the truck," she said, ignoring the catch in her voice. "They're bound to be coming soon."

She hadn't realized Jack had been hugging her until she tried to nudge him toward the passenger side of the truck. His hands remained on her waist for a moment, his fingers splaying down toward her hips and his mouth still quirked in a lopsided smile. "Those jerks aren't going to be going anywhere soon," he said.

"How do you know that?"

"They've got a couple of very, very flat tires." He reached into the front pocket of his trousers and pulled out a pocketknife. "Think you're the only one with a weapon?"

"You slashed their tires?"

"Just two. But assuming they've only got one spare..."

She allowed herself a slight smile. Jack Slater was a clever man.

And he had the diamonds in his pocket. *Her* diamonds.

"Get in," she said coolly, gesturing toward the cab. "Maybe you've got a knife and I've got a gun. What we don't have, Mr. Slater, is a plan."

Evidently he could hear the aloofness in her tone. His smile grew chilly as he measured her with his gaze. Without another word, he let go of her and climbed into the truck. After putting his knife away, he tucked his hand into the pocket with the diamonds. There it remained, protective, possessive, as she shifted into gear and continued along the winding road.

Chapter Three

"Diamonds!" Jessie Harlon shook his head. "Honest to God, Mandy, how do these things happen to you?"

Jack studied Mandy's brother over the rim of his glass. Like Mandy, Jessie Harlon was slim of build and endowed with a mane of wild red hair, but what on Mandy looked ravishingly beautiful, on her brother looked almost comical.

Not that Jack would ever think anything negative about the man who'd taken him into his house, given him a swift inspection, declared, "You look like you could use some liquid refreshment," and handed him a glass filled with a generous dose of bourbon.

"Nothing happened to me," Mandy grumbled, adding another half inch of bourbon to the scant portion Jessie had poured for her. "All I know is I ordered quartz and this is what I got." She gestured toward the sack sitting in the middle of the round pine table like some misbegotten centerpiece.

Jack observed the graceful motion of her hand as she waved toward the bag, and then as she lifted her glass to her lips. He'd been observing her hands and her lips ever since he'd taken his seat beside her in the cab of her truck. He'd noticed the way concentration tensed her mouth, the way her teeth played over the fullness of her lower lip as she navigated the twisting mountain roads. He'd noticed her deft manipulation of the gear stick, her palm molded over its black plastic knob, her fingers curling sensuously around it.

He'd wanted to talk to her then, before they reached wherever they were going. He'd wanted to question her about the two strangers, about her supplier. About whether she had a boyfriend. About whether, once this whole incident was over, he could interest her in a night on the town, dinner, bed . . . whatever.

Such thoughts were out of line, and out of whack. Mandy Harlon was a hillbilly doll maker. Jack was a New York City businessman. And there was nothing he'd rather do than return to New York and business as usual.

With the Moe doll, though. He didn't want to go back without the Moe doll.

"Your supplier sent you that," Jessie was saying with a nod at the sack of stones, "and then he sent two goons after you to get the diamonds. Seems a mite convoluted to me."

It didn't seem at all convoluted to Jack. "The supplier is a smuggler," he said, stating the obvious. "The guy's trying to smuggle gems in from Brazil. He can't ship them directly to himself, so he stashes them with a bunch of quartz and addresses the shipment to Mandy, who nobody would ever suspect of anything. Then he sends the goons to find her and get the stuff from her. They wander into the Sunnyside Café just about when I happen to be asking directions to Mandy's house. They overhear the directions, follow me up the mountain and decide to check out my doll for diamonds before they bother with her. And not realizing who they're dealing with, they blow their mission." For effect, Jack tipped his bourbon glass. "That's what happened."

Mandy and her brother gaped at him. "You've worked it out pretty neatly, haven't you?" she said.

"They looked familiar to me," Jack explained. "I couldn't figure out why until I heard them talking in your kitchen. I must have seen them at the Sunnyside Café when I was asking for directions to your house."

Mandy traced the rim of her glass with her index finger. He recalled the feel of those hands on his face, swabbing his cuts. And the feel of her arms around him when he'd climbed down from the back of her truck.

If only her brother weren't sitting right there, Jack would give in to temptation, haul her onto his lap and kiss her. Not because she seemed to invite such a move, not because she'd done anything to indicate an interest in him, but because... because she was unbearably sexy. Tough, flinty, talented and pretty, and that sultry drawl of hers, and those silky hands of hers . . .

He took another swig of bourbon and focused on her brother.

"It seems simple enough," Jessie opined, leaning back in his chair until he could reach the pack of cigarettes on the counter behind him. He shook one out and lit it, then extended the box to Jack, who declined. "Why don't you just give the creeps the diamonds and send them on their way?"

"The creeps already have diamonds," Jack argued. "They've got my Moe doll."

"They've also got a gun," Mandy reminded him.

"So do you. I want my doll. I paid for it. It's mine."

"I could make you another one, if that's what's bothering you."

There was no way Jack would sit around waiting for her to sew another doll.

Besides, the one she'd made was filled with diamonds. Jack had paid for it, which made the diamonds his.

By the same token, the diamonds in the drawstring bag at the center of the table were Mandy's. "I don't think you should give the creeps anything," he said. "You paid for the shipment. It's yours."

She gazed at the bag and shuddered. "I'm not sure a sack of diamonds is worth getting killed for."

A knock on the front door interrupted them. Jessie sent a meaningful look to Jack and Mandy, then exhaled a long stream of smoke and lumbered out of the room. Mandy grabbed the bag and searched the room for a place to stash it. As she heard the front door open, she tossed the bag into the freezer and leaned against the white enamel door to close it.

"Bill!" Jessie boomed from the parlor. "What brings you around these parts?"

Mandy blanched. "Bill McIntyre," she whispered to Jack.

"Who's Bill McIntyre?" Jack whispered back.

"How's it going, Jessie?" came Bill's voice. "Tell ya the truth, I'm lookin' for ya baby sister. I seen her truck outside, and I reckon she must be 'round here someplace."

Mandy cursed under her breath, then managed a weak smile for the bulky, brawny man who suddenly filled the kitchen doorway. He wore a khaki uniform and a gun in a leather holster around his hips. His face was puffy, his cheeks pink, and his nose absurdly small, his eyes fringed with tiny lashes a few shades lighter than his thinning gray-blond hair.

A sheriff? Jack guessed. A state trooper?

"Why, hello there, peaches," Bill greeted Mandy with a flirtatious wink. Mandy pursed her lips in distaste. "I been lookin' for you."

"Well you found me," she snapped. Her cheeks grew rosy with a blush of discomfort.

"I hear tell there was a bit of an altercation at your house not more'n a half hour ago." Bill McIntyre hooked his thumbs around his holster and turned his scrutiny to Jack. "And who might you be?"

"I might be anyone," Jack answered dryly. He decided he didn't like Bill McIntyre. He'd never been fond of law-enforcement types. This particular representative of the breed, with his milky skin, his gill-round cheeks and his watery, bulging eyes, made Jack think of a fish. An overweight, unrefrigerated cod.

"Well, you surely do fit the description I got from a couple of gentlemen visiting our fine town who say you vandalized their car."

"I did what?"

Bill's smile grew predatory. "Mind if I search your pockets, son?"

"Yes, I do mind," Jack said, meeting his accusing stare directly.

"Well, now, you know and I know there's a knife in your pocket. I suppose I can obtain a search warrant, if that's what you want me to do. Search warrant takes time, though. Days, maybe. Meanwhile, I'll have to hold you on probable cause till we can get old Judge Warner to issue me a warrant. Tell me, Mandy, punkin," Bill McIntyre continued, turning back to her, "how come you're entertaining the likes of this fella when you know he's got a knife in his pocket?"

"What's wrong with having a knife?" she said. "Lots of people have them."

"Lots of people don't use them to cut holes in tires. Come on, son. Why don't you-all empty your pockets now?"

Hearing the cop call him "son" was enough to make Jack want to use his knife on the blubbery spare tire riding above Bill's belt. Moe was the only person in the world entitled to call Jack "son," and he didn't. Which was one more reason Jack loved him.

On the other hand, he'd rather produce his knife than have Bill McIntyre obtain a search warrant and go through all of Jack's things. Sighing, he pulled himself to his feet and removed his penknife from his pocket.

Bill made a big production of covering his hand with a handkerchief before he touched the knife, as if he wanted to preserve the fingerprints on it. "You got a license to carry this thing?" he asked Jack.

"It's a pocketknife, for crying out loud."

"Well, you're charged with first-degree vandalism. Damage to property. I'm gonna have to run you in."

Mandy's cheeks grew even darker, flushed with rage. "Bill, don't be ridiculous."

"Ain't being ridiculous, sweetheart. Just doing my job."

"For the first time in ages," she muttered under her breath. Louder, she said, "Before you run him anywhere, I've got to take care of his injuries."

Jack almost protested that the scratches on his face were superficial. Then he understood that she was simply stalling the officer.

"We'll be right back," she said. "Come on, Jack, let me tape those cuts." She padded in her bare feet out of the kitchen and up the stairs. Jack followed, ignoring Bill McIntyre's oily stare.

"You-all better not try anything fancy," Bill shouted after them.

"Like what?" Mandy shouted back, already halfway up the stairs. "Escaping over the roof?"

"That's right. I swear I'll get the entire county sheriff's office down here if—"

"Don't worry about it," Jack assured him, his tone acidic. "I don't do roofs."

At the top of the stairs, Mandy grabbed Jack's elbow and hustled him down the hall into a minuscule bathroom under the eaves. The ceiling sloped so precipitously he bumped his head on it. She quickly lowered the toilet seat for him to sit on, then shut and locked the door.

It was a tight fit for the two of them. Jack spread his legs, propping one against the wall and extending the other under the sink, so Mandy could stand between them. She didn't have to stretch to reach the medicine cabinet, from which she pulled a box of adhesive bandage strips and a bottle of antiseptic.

His eyes were level with her chest. If he shifted forward and angled his head, he could press his lips into the hollow between her small, high breasts. He could ring his arms around her waist and pull her to him.

For safety's sake, he closed his eyes and leaned back against the tank. When she touched a cotton swab to his cheek, he flinched at the sudden burning sensation along his cut.

"Listen to me." She spoke softly, urgently. "Bill McIntyre's an ass. He can be bought."

"Bought?" Jack opened his eyes and found himself gazing up into Mandy's. The astonishing blue of her irises momentarily stunned him. "Are you suggesting that I bribe him?"

"I'm suggesting—" she dabbed the cheek again, then brushed the hair off his brow and dabbed the cut there "—that the goons might have bribed him."

"You think they bribed him to arrest me?"

"Most probably."

"What do you think I should do?"

She tossed the cotton into the sink and peered down at him. If he wanted, he could interpret her expression as genuine concern.

She was under no obligation to worry about him. She had her diamonds and his check. His fate ought to be irrelevant to her.

For whatever reason, though, she cared about what happened to him. "Go with Bill and keep your mouth shut. I'll arrange for bail."

"Bail?" he erupted.

She pressed her hand against his mouth to stifle him. Her fingers smelled not of antiseptic but of bourbon and rain. It took all his willpower not to slide out his tongue and lure them between his teeth.

"I'm not going to leave you to rot in jail, Mr. Slater," she vowed.

He had to laugh at her formality. Her body was less than an inch from his, trapped between his thighs, and her hand was draped seductively across his lips and chin, and she was calling him Mr. Slater. "Call me Jack."

"Jack."

"I'm not going to jail," he said. "What does this guy have on me? If the goons charge me with slashing their tires, I'll charge them with theft and attempted murder. I'll—"

"Listen to me." She stared into his eyes for a moment longer, then broke away and reached for the box of bandage strips. "This isn't New York City. This is Harrow, Kentucky. We've got an empty jail cell and a bored police officer. He's gonna want to keep himself busy with you for as long as he can. It'll make him feel important."

"There are laws—"

"Harrow has its own laws," she murmured, applying a bandage to his forehead. Her hand moved over the adhesive, smoothing it, her fingers as soft and light as daisy petals. "You let me and Jessie get you out of there."

"Why should I trust you?" he asked.

"You don't have much choice."

Her hand stilled on his brow and she gazed down at him. Her eyes were so clear, so beautiful. White and blue, surrounded by the thick red fringe of her lashes. How could he not trust something so utterly red, white and blue?

Without considering the consequences, he lifted his hands to her narrow waist. She started slightly, but she didn't back away. Maybe she couldn't, maybe there wasn't enough space in the bathroom, but she let him hold her waist as he'd held it when they'd stood next to her truck at the side of the road.

"Whatever you do," she reminded him in a surprisingly breathless voice, "don't tell Bill about the diamonds."

"They're probably stolen. Contraband."

"I know." Her thumb moved along his hairline. He felt his scalp tighten from the sensation, and the muscles in his thighs clench with pleasure.

"What are you going to do with them while I'm up in the big house?" he asked. His whole body was doing a slow burn.

She smiled briefly, nervously, as if she knew what he was feeling. As if she was feeling it, too. "I don't know," she murmured, daring to let her fingers wander into his hair. "Maybe leave them in Jessie's freezer awhile."

"Might as well. Stolen diamonds are called ice."

"And I'll try to get your doll for you."

"No. Don't go back to your house without me. Those guys—"

"I'll bring Jessie with me."

"And your rifle?"

"And my *shotgun*." She smiled at him, a longer, surer smile.

He couldn't keep from sliding his hands up her back to her shoulders, to her throat, to her cheeks. Framing her face, he mirrored her smile. "Someday you've got to explain the difference to me."

She nodded, swallowed, moistened her lips with the tip of her tongue. Her eyes never left him.

He started to pull her down to him. Just one kiss, he swore to himself. Just a brief good-luck kiss, because they trusted each other, because she was going to help him and he was grateful. Because he couldn't resist those lush pink lips of hers another second.

Suddenly, Bill McIntyre hollered up the stairs, "Get it in gear, Mandy-kins. I want my prisoner!"

Mandy broke from Jack and opened the bathroom door. Jack let his hands fall and released the breath he hadn't realized he was holding.

"He's ready," she called down.

No, he's not, Jack thought, although he kept quiet. He wasn't ready to march off to some jail cell with a jerk like Bill McIntyre. More important, he wasn't ready to let go of Mandy Harlon.

But she was out in the hall, starting down the stairs. He saw no option but to follow her down and hand himself over to Harrow, Kentucky's allegedly bribable officer of the peace.

THE JAIL—in fact, the entire municipal government of Harrow, Kentucky—was located in a small, nondescript building across Main Street from the Sunnyside Café. Entering the single room that housed Harrow's police department and holding cell, Jack recalled his one miserable foray into the police station in downtown Troy, New York, when he'd been a kid desperate for help and had instead been delivered right back into the horror he'd been trying to escape. Ever since that time, he'd exerted himself to steer clear of the police.

Now here he was, in a small town far from home, being fingerprinted by a mousy, whisper-voiced clerk while Bill McIntyre strutted his stuff around the room. "You-all shoulda stayed in New York, where you belong," he scolded, looking damned proud of himself. "We don't like no tire slashers around here."

Jack longed to tell Officer McIntyre why he'd chosen to slash the tires of his adversaries. He'd been fighting for his life, for God's sake, his life and Mandy's.

But Mandy had cautioned Jack to keep his mouth shut, and he heeded her warning. If the goons had in fact bribed Bill McIntyre, reciting a list of their transgressions wasn't going to do Jack any good.

Instead he said, "I believe I'm entitled to a phone call."

Bill eyed him askance. Evidently he wasn't used to prisoners knowing their rights. "You-all haven't been formally charged with anything yet."

"Then charge me and let me make my call."

Bill stared at Jack. Jack stared back. Bill faltered. "Let him use the phone, Lucy," he said to the clerk, who scurried to her desk and indicated her telephone with a mute, meek wave.

Jack crossed to the desk, made himself comfortable in the chair, and dialed Moe's number in New York.

"Jack!" Moe squawked once Jack had identified himself. "Hi! Where are you? Still in Tennessee?"

"Kentucky," Jack corrected him.

"Tennessee, Kentucky, what's the difference? So, you'll be back tomorrow?"

Jack sighed wistfully. Moe's gravelly voice made him homesick for the city. "I don't know when I'll be back, Moe. I've kind of run into a problem."

"A problem? What? The doll isn't ready? I've got to tell you, Jack, Steven Barton at the club—he humiliated me in handball yesterday. Jack, I don't know if I can show my face there ever again, the way he wiped the floor with me. Anyway, he told me his sister got one of those rose-quartz dolls for her daughter at Dido last year, and the daughter got a combined score of over fifteen hundred on her SATs. I don't remember the exact number, Jack, but over fifteen hundred. She's going to Cornell. All from this doll, Jack. If a doll can get Steve Barton's niece into Cornell, don't you think it can get my fingers to straighten out?"

No, actually, I don't, Jack wanted to say. But he would never deprive Moe of hope.

"So, Jack, you've got my doll?"

"Not quite," Jack answered. "The thing is, Moe, I, uh, I kind of got into a scrape with the local police down here."

"The police? Jack, come on! You're a big boy. What, you broke the speed limit?"

"Well, it's a little more complicated than that. I can't really go into details, because there's a cop standing here listening to my every word." He glared at Bill McIntyre, who showed absolutely no remorse over his flagrant eavesdropping.

"Okay, okay." Moe fell silent for a moment. "So. You need a lawyer? I could send someone down."

"I don't think so. I can probably straighten this thing out before it comes to that. I just wanted to let you know. I'm not sure when I'll be getting back to New York."

"Here's an idea—use the doll. Make a wish and get yourself out of this mess. The quartz crystals will help you."

"The doll is yours, Moe."

"I'm letting you use it. Use up the magic if you have to. Just get yourself out of trouble."

Jack couldn't bring himself to reveal that he didn't have the doll, didn't even know where it was. And he wasn't going to insult Moe by telling him he had no faith in the power of a heap of stones, even if some of them happened to be diamonds. "I'm not going to use up the magic, Moe," he insisted. "The doll was custom-designed for you, for your arthritis. Let's save it for that."

"All right, well, listen. You behave yourself. They're all meshuga rednecks down there—"

"And you're a meshuga New Yorker," Jack said indulgently. "I'll be fine."

"You need someone to help you out, someone who knows the territory...."

A memory of Mandy Harlon came to life inside him: her lush red hair, her full, soft lips, the slender span of her waist in his hands, the whisper of her fingertips against his forehead. *Why should I trust you?* he had asked, and she'd answered, *You don't have much choice.*

"I've got someone," he assured Moe. "I'll be all right."

"Take care, Jack. I worry about you."

"I know. It gives you something to do. I'll keep you posted, Moe." He hung up and met Bill's nosy grin. "Now what?"

"Now," Bill drawled, "we're gonna lock you up for a while." He led Jack to the tiny holding cell, ushered him inside with a flourish, and then stepped out and locked the door.

Jack stared at the grim steel bars that separated him from the small office. He watched Lucy the clerk flit around, looking frenzied, jumping whenever Bill spoke to her. He checked his watch—nearly five o'clock—and thought about Mandy.

And worried.

Why would the thugs bribe McIntyre to lock up Jack, other than to make sure Jack stayed out of their way? They were probably tearing apart Mandy's house right now, searching for the diamonds. If Mandy walked in on them, what would they do to her? They wouldn't kill her, not before they had the jewels.

If anything happened to her...

He deliberately shoved the idea out of his mind. In its place another idea took hold—that Mandy would take her diamonds and disappear. They must be worth millions. By now, for all Jack knew, she was buying a one-way ticket to some South Sea island, where she would live out the rest of her days in luxurious anonymity.

Meanwhile, Jack would be doing a life sentence in a dreary holding cell in downtown Harrow.

She'd promised, though. She'd promised not to leave him to rot in jail.

Damn. He should have accepted Moe's offer to send down a lawyer.

But he didn't want a lawyer. He wanted Mandy. He wanted her to waltz into the one-room police station with Jack's doll tucked under her arm and *two* tickets to the South Sea island.

He wanted her to live up to his trust.

He looked at his watch again: ten minutes past five. He sank onto a splintered wooden bench beneath the tiny barred window and closed his eyes.

A South Sea island. Palm trees, white sand, the ocean as blue as Mandy's eyes, her body burnished to a golden glow by the sun. They would make love on the beach, in the frothing surf, in the shade of a coral grotto. They would feed each other bananas, drink coconut milk, cash in a diamond or two to build a windmill to generate electricity for the stereo system, so they could listen to good jazz whenever they wanted. . . .

"Let him out, Bill."

At the sound of that strong female voice Jack bolted upright and opened his eyes. Leaping to his feet, he raced to the bars and peered around the bend to see Mandy entering the room.

"Mandy. Sweetheart." Bill greeted her with an unctuous smile.

"Either show me a sworn complaint against him or let him out."

"A sworn complaint? Now, Mandy—"

"Do it, Bill," she ordered him. "The law says you can't hold him on someone's word."

"Don't you go throwing the law in my face, Mandy. I got justifiable cause to hold him."

"And I got Clark Devins down at the Texaco station who tells me there's all sorts of things that can slash a tire. Big knives, little knives, kitchen knives, X-Actos, scissors, pruning shears, a hand ax... Should I keep going?"

"Well, I reckon it might take a forensic examination to ascertain—"

"Don't use words you don't understand, Bill. Let Mr. Slater out of that holding cell or you'll be facing a civil suit."

Bill glared at her for a pregnant moment, then dug a key out of his pocket and unlocked the cell door.

Jack stepped outside. He wanted to scoop Mandy into his arms and swing her around, and thank her not just for getting him out but for living up to his trust in her. That impulse was tempered by his awe at her ability to cow the burly cop.

"You're on my list, Miss Amanda Harlon," Bill warned, wagging a threatening finger at Mandy.

She responded with a sugary smile. "And you're on mine, Officer William McIntyre."

She and Jack stepped outside into the chilly, drizzly evening. Her black pickup was parked in front of the municipal building. Jack's gaze strayed past it to the café across the street. He realized he was starving.

"Get in," she said, swinging open the driver's side door of the truck.

They could talk about dinner later. Right now he owed her his unquestioning compliance. He climbed into the cab beside her and scrutinized the bulky leather purse she carried.

"Where'd you come up with all that legal jargon?" he asked admiringly.

She cruised down the main street, passing the café, a general store, a Texaco station and a hardware store as they left the heart of town. "I called an old boyfriend of mine. He's a lawyer. He gave me some fancy phrases to throw around."

An old boyfriend. An old boyfriend who was a lawyer. "Is he from around here?" he asked. "We might find we need a good attorney."

She shook her head. "He lives in Atlanta."

"Ah." So many important issues to consider, and all Jack could think about was that Mandy used to date a lawyer in Atlanta.

Used to. Past tense.

"It was nice of him to help out," said Jack, hoping she would elaborate on the specifics of the relationship.

"We're friends," she said laconically.

Jack wondered whether he and Mandy could wind up friends—and, if so, whether they could get to be something more than friends first. "What's in your purse?" he asked.

"The diamonds, among other things."

"And the doll?"

"No. I'm sorry. It wasn't at my house. They ransacked the place, Jack, they just..." Her voice wavered and then broke; he noticed the flutter in her throat as she swallowed. "I couldn't leave the diamonds at Jessie's. They're sure to head there next."

"So where are we going?"

"I don't know." She swallowed again, blinked, and turned right at the end of the street. "You may as well go back to New York. There's nothing for you here."

"There's my doll."

She sighed. "They've got your doll, Jack. How the hell do you think you're gonna get it from them?"

"You've got the diamonds. They're sure to come after them, and—"

"Oh, swell. I'm the bait. You're gonna dangle me in front of their noses to get your stupid doll?"

"Have you got a better idea?"

"Yeah. Kiss the doll goodbye. I'll make you another one."

"And meanwhile, what happens to all those diamonds?" He looked at the purse on the floor near his feet.

Her mouth opened and then shut. She flicked on her headlights, her windshield wipers. "I haven't figured that out yet. I've got to put some distance between me and those creeps, and then I'll decide."

"Let's go to Huntington," he suggested.

"West Virginia?"

"I've got a motel room there. We can get something to eat and think things through."

"You want me to go to a motel room with you?"

"To think," he emphasized. "And eat." At her silence, he added, "I left my suitcase there, my stuff. Besides, those creeps won't find us there."

She remained silent.

"The most important thing right now," he emphasized, "is for you to figure out what you're going to do with the diamonds."

"All right," she muttered, then jerked the steering wheel to the right, following the sign to Route 23. They drove north, through the rain, through the hills, heading for West Virginia.

And the next most important thing to do, he thought, was to figure out how far he and Mandy were willing to trust each other.

Chapter Four

Never go to a motel room with a strange man.

That was one of Mandy's mother's commandments, along with never stepping out in torn underwear, never kissing a boy on the first date, and never wearing white shoes before Memorial Day or after Labor Day. That last one had always baffled Mandy, whose only white footwear as a child had been canvas gym sneakers.

Mandy's mother lived under the delusion that because she was originally from Louisville, she was actually a fine, properly bred lady who had, through some bizarre twist of fate, wound up married to a rube from the Kentucky hill country. Not that she didn't love Mandy's father—she was truly quite crazy about him—but as Gramma Harlon used to say, "Yer mama sure do put on airs."

Nonetheless, as Mandy gazed around her at Jack Slater's motel room, she found herself wondering whether her mother had been right—at least about motel rooms.

He was taking a shower. Through the bathroom door she could hear the constant rush of water, echoing in the shower stall, occasionally interrupted by a syncopated splatter when he stepped under the spray. Those splatters conjured up visions of him soaping his body and rinsing it.

His body. Clean, wet . . . naked.

Forget the warnings about motel rooms. Mandy's mother should have taught her never to think about what the sexiest man in the world would look like taking a shower.

She distracted herself by studying her surroundings. There was nothing threatening in the room. Nothing but the usual motel decor: indestructible furniture, trite artwork bolted to the walls, a color television, more heavy glass ashtrays than the most fanatical chain-smoker could possibly require, and a single queen-size bed.

Nothing threatening? Ha.

She sat gingerly on the edge of the bed, hugging her purse to her. Jack had already telephoned Moe Kaplan; now it was her turn to call her brother.

"Where the heck are you?" Jessie asked once Mandy had said hello.

"West Virginia," she said, bracing herself for his reaction.

He swore under his breath. "Why are you in West Virginia?"

"Because Jack has—" she swallowed "—a motel room here."

Instead of swearing this time, Jessie laughed. "Making the best of a bad situation, are you?"

"I'm doing no such thing."

"Well, you ought to. You've got billions of dollars' worth of diamonds in your bag—"

"Millions, not billions—"

"And a good-lookin' young stud to keep you company—"

"He's not ... a stud," she finished lamely. She couldn't very well say he wasn't good-looking. "As far as his keeping me company goes, I reckon he's just sticking around because of those millions of dollars' worth of diamonds."

Jessie was still chuckling. "Honey, there's some men who'll chase a lady for her money, and some who'll chase her for something quite else. I'd wager a week's supply of Wild Turkey your friend Jack don't fall into the first category."

It was a bet Mandy wasn't about to take. She heard the shower shut off, suffered a brief, vivid mental flash of Jack stepping out of the stall, his body shimmering with residual moisture...and banished the image from her mind. "I just wanted to pass along the phone number here, in case you need to reach me. We'll be here till we figure out where we're heading next."

"A man don't have to be a rocket scientist to figure out where you two are headin'," Jessie teased. "I saw the way he was lookin' at you—and the way you were lookin' at him. Just be careful, Mandy. You've been out of circulation a long time. You're likely a bit rusty.''

"Might I remind you," she snapped, "that after the divorce you and Iris went through, you're in no position to give me any advice whatsoever." She heard a click as the bathroom door opened. "I've gotta go, Jessie. Whatever you do, don't let Bill know where we are. Or those thugs."

"If I see those thugs, I'll be too busy wringin' their necks to tell them where you are." Jessie's voice took on a solemn tone. "You be careful, Mandy. I mean that."

She hung up in time to see Jack step into the room. He had on a clean pair of jeans—and nothing else. The towel hanging around his neck did nothing to hide the supple contours of his torso, slick, gold-hued skin tapering down past a flat abdomen to the low-slung edge of his jeans. His shoulders were thick, and hard muscles shaped his upper arms. He had no chest hair. Only smooth, damp skin, flat brown nipples.

She lowered her eyes, thinking she'd be safer if she concentrated on what he was wearing rather than what he wasn't wearing. But her attention lingered only for a moment on his legs before rising to the unevenly faded blue denim covering his fly.

"Did you want to wash up?" he asked.

She gulped and forced her gaze to his face. His hair was wet, his eyes bright. He had removed the bandages from his cheek and forehead, exposing long, dark gashes.

She rose and crossed the room to inspect his injuries. He hadn't shaved—a razor would no doubt have aggravated the wound on his cheek. She touched it gently to make sure it hadn't opened up again.

He stopped breathing for a moment, then covered her hand with his and eased it from his skin. "I'll live."

"It looks worse than before."

"I scab ugly." He turned away, presenting her with a magnificent view of his strong, smooth back as he rummaged through the open suitcase on the dresser and pulled out a fresh shirt. She was relieved, but also a little disappointed, when he put it on. He didn't turn back to her until all the buttons were done, as if he wanted to spare her the disturbing sight of his bare chest. Even clothed, he looked too handsome.

"I'll just go rinse my face," she said, fleeing into the bathroom.

The air was humid, the mirror layered with fog. She splashed cold water on her cheeks. That was what she needed: to stay cool and composed. She couldn't afford to let Jack Slater steam her up and blur her thoughts the way his shower had steamed and blurred the mirror.

After few more splashes of icy water, she wasn't thinking about him at all. She was thinking about her purse out in the bedroom, with the sack of diamonds inside it. It didn't matter how attractive she found Jack; she shouldn't have trusted him alone with her bag.

She yanked open the door and spied her purse lying exactly where she'd left it on the bed. Jack was staring out the window at the motel parking lot. He spun around at the sound of her entrance.

"I'm starving," he said. "Why don't we grab something to eat?"

She strode directly to the bed to collect her purse, then joined him at the front door. He smelled of soap and shampoo and freshly laundered clothing. After the muggy heat of the bathroom, the bedroom felt chilly—but when she passed close to him, she felt hot again. Steamy.

She hurried outside. The sidewalk bordering the parking lot was protected by an overhang. Beyond it she could see the rain coming down hard. The sky was a dark purple, and the air had lost what little springtime warmth it held earlier.

Jack checked to make sure the door was locked, then took her arm and escorted her down the sheltered sidewalk, past a dozen numbered doors to the coffee shop. His fingers cupped her elbow casually, as if this was just a bit of etiquette he did without thinking. Yet her entire arm tingled from the contact.

A man don't have to be a rocket scientist to figure out where you two are headin', Jessie had said. Well, damn it, just because she was overreacting to Jack's light touch didn't mean she was heading anywhere with him, other than to the coffee shop for some victuals. If she happened to be just a bit too aware of him as a man, it was only because, as Jessie had reminded her, she'd been out of circulation a long time. And she'd unexpectedly found herself in possession of a fortune in diamonds, and a jerk with a revolver had fired at her truck, and her house had been ransacked....

She was entitled to be a little crazy at this point.

A sudden gust of damp evening air blew her and Jack into the coffee shop. He released her arm to shove his wind-tossed hair off his face. As soon as they were seated, he opened the menu and sighed. "I haven't eaten since breakfast," he said.

"I reckon driving off a cliff can surely build up an appetite in a man."

He peered at her over the edge of his menu and chuckled. "It most surely can," he confirmed, trying to imitate her drawl and doing a shabby job of it. He flagged a waitress over and ordered a bowl of soup, a club steak and a large cola on ice.

Mandy hadn't had much time to study the menu, so she asked only for a chicken sandwich. The waitress filled their glasses with water and then removed their menus, depriving Mandy of her shield. Now she had no choice but to look at Jack.

He was something to look at. Even with his day-old shadow of beard, with his angry cuts and his damp, mussed hair, his toffee brown eyes and his alluring smile...

"Who's Moe?" she asked, hoping to distract her thoughts.

Jack settled back in his chair and regarded her thoughtfully. "The short answer is, he's my father." He sipped the soft drink the waitress had delivered, then eyed her and smiled. "Foster father," he answered her unspoken question.

Jack's past was none of her business. But curiosity got the better of her. "You must love him very much, chasing all the way down here and risking life and limb to get him his doll."

"When I chased all the way down here," Jack said with a wry smile, "I thought all I was risking was a couple of days away from my office."

"Office?" She couldn't picture Jack in a suit, issuing orders from a huge mahogany desk. He seemed much too... physical, somehow. "What sort of work do you do?"

"Business supplies. Moe founded the company. Of course, now we're more into computers." He described their services, from Moe's early days—when the company sold paper clips and rubber bands—to the present, when, under Jack's management, the firm designed software systems and staff training programs. "So, you see, we're quite diverse." He took another sip of soda and grinned sheepishly. "I'm boring you."

"No," she said quickly. She loved hearing him tell her about what he did—and, indeed, she could more easily see Jack lying on the floor hooking up computer components than shipping orders of paper clips. "So, you work for Moe Kaplan?"

"He's retired now. After I proved to him that I could run the business better than he could, he turned it over to me."

"That's mighty generous."

Jack shrugged. "I was the son he never had. He was the father I never had. We were a good fit." His soup had arrived, and he gave it a desultory stir before lifting a spoonful to his lips. His gaze met hers and he hesitated. "What? You don't believe me?"

She must have looked as bemused as she felt. "It's just...well, you said he's your foster father. And then, to turn his business over to you..."

"I guess he likes me," he joked, then consumed some soup. His smile faded. "Really, Moe was more of a father to me than my own father."

"What about your mother?"

"She died when I was nine." His eyes never left Mandy as he ate his soup. She supposed that if her questions bothered him he would tell her to shut up.

"So your father turned you over to foster parents?"

"Not exactly." He leaned back in his chair, the uneven tapping of his index finger against the edge of the table the only sign that he was at all uncomfortable. "My father had problems with self-control. That's a fancy social services way of saying he drank too much and got violent. He loved my mother, and her death pushed him over the edge." He took a sip of soda. "The first time he walloped me, I went to the police. They were great—they called my father and told him to come and get me." A bitter laugh escaped him. "The next time it happened, I knew better than to go to the police. I ran away."

"I see." She felt sorry for him. In her life, home was a place she came back to, not a place she needed to escape. She'd enjoyed living in Atlanta, but when Gramma Harlon became ill a few years ago, her parents were living in Arizona, and Jessie and Iris were in the middle of their contentious divorce. So Mandy had said goodbye to the big city, her friends and Bobby Lee, who to this day couldn't understand why an attractive single woman would want to sequester herself in the Appalachian backwoods. But Mandy had come back to Harrow without a second thought.

"I hitchhiked to Manhattan," Jack went on. "One night I chose to stay warm in Moe Kaplan's doorway. It was February. I was freezing. He took me inside and gave me something to eat."

"He sounds like a wonderful man."

Jack's smile lost its bittersweet cast. "He's the sort of man I'd risk life and limb and all the rest of it for, just to get him a doll. He's got arthritis. His fingers are all gnarled up. He thinks the rose-quartz crystals inside the doll are going to cure him."

Mandy felt inadequate and not a little guilty. Her dolls couldn't work miracles.

"Of course, Moe's doll isn't stuffed with quartz," Jack noted. "It's stuffed with diamonds, so who knows what it can cure."

"Jack." She fell silent as the waitress delivered their food. As soon as they were alone once more, she said, "A bottle of aspirin would do more for Moe Kaplan's hands than any doll I could make. The dolls are fun, they give people a cause for hope, but they don't cure arthritis."

"Moe believes they might."

"And here you are, getting shot at because of it. It's just not worth it, Jack. I'll make Moe another doll. It's not worth getting yourself killed."

He chuckled and dug into his steak. "Make Moe another doll if you want. But I paid for the original one. It's mine. And even if it doesn't cure Moe's arthritis, the stones inside that doll could pay for an awful lot of aspirin."

She nibbled on her sandwich. Her bag lay heavy in her lap. How many aspirin could the diamonds inside buy? How much of anything?

"Do you really think the diamonds were smuggled in from Brazil?" she asked, recalling the theory Jack had outlined at Jessie's house.

"As opposed to . . . ?"

"I don't know." She picked at the crust of her bread with her thumb until a shred tore off. "Maybe they got delivered to me by mistake."

"If it were just a mistake, the goons would have shown up on your doorstep like gentlemen, documented the error, apologized for the inconvenience and taken the diamonds with them when they left. They wouldn't have tried to kill us."

"I reckon there are some things worth being killed over. But diamonds aren't it. If I could just get the diamonds back to the goons, they'd go away and leave me be."

"That would only work if they were reasonable human beings. It's obvious they aren't."

"But—"

"And, anyway, the diamonds are yours. You paid for the shipment, you accepted it, it's yours. Nobody can prove what was in that carton but you. You're the only one who saw it."

"*You* saw it."

"Fine. If you want to share the diamonds with me, I'd be happy to oblige."

"I'll bet," she muttered, tucking her free hand securely around the bag in her lap. She realized she wasn't quite ready to turn over the diamonds to anyone—not the thugs, not the authorities, not even Jack. He was right. They were hers. No one's but hers.

She hugged the bag more tightly to herself.

Before she could reach for her wallet, Jack paid the bill. She tamped down the suspicion that he was figuring on having her pay her part of the tab later on, in hundreds of carat weight. Assuming the worst of him wasn't going to help her. So far, he'd proven himself to be on her side.

The rain had relaxed into a steady drizzle during their meal. The few lights illuminating the parking lot glared against the wet, black asphalt; the air had lost its nippiness. As Mandy and Jack strolled back to his room, she realized that they hadn't yet figured out what they were going to do.

She also realized that she was exhausted. The food warmed her belly and reminded her of how much had happened since Jack Slater had walked through her door that afternoon.

What tired her more than anything else was her constant attraction to him, and her unflagging vigilance in resisting that attraction. Desiring a man she had no business desiring, and then laboring to ignore that desire, could drain a woman of energy.

By the time he'd unlocked the door to his room, all she wanted to do was lie down on the bed. Alone. They could work out their strategy later, after she'd rested a bit.

"You look beat," Jack observed before she could say anything.

"I am beat."

He gestured toward the bed. "Take a load off."

"What are you going to do?"

"Pack a little," he said, crossing to his open suitcase. "Catch some news on the tube. See if there are any known jewel thieves on the loose in eastern Kentucky." At her dubious frown, he added, "Seriously, Mandy—get some rest. Who knows what we'll be facing tomorrow."

"I thought we were going to work out a plan," she said, sitting on the bed and yanking off her shoes.

"You're not going to work out anything. You're asleep on your feet."

"I'm not on my feet," she argued, nestling her head into the pillow and extending her legs. She cradled her purse in her arms and felt her eyelids slide shut. "Don't make any plans without me" were her last words before sleep blanketed her in sweet darkness.

JACK DELIBERATELY avoided looking at the bed. If he so much as glanced at her, the temptation would be too great. And he didn't want to be tempted.

Mandy Harlon was clearly much more enamored of her diamonds than she was of him. Look at what she'd taken to bed with her. Look at what she was cuddling to her bosom: that big leather bag of hers.

He gathered his things inside his suitcase in case he had to make a quick getaway, and then turned the television on low. The sound bothered Mandy, who moaned quietly in her sleep and rolled over, bringing her precious bag with her.

West Virginia television seemed to be just as crummy as New York television: same stupid shows, same stupid advertisements. He'd ride it out till a news break and see if they ran a report on gun-toting baddies in Harrow, Kentucky.

Not that his escapades of that afternoon would be deemed worthy of coverage. Hell, in New York you had to be murdered to have even a remote chance of making the news.

At least the television offered a diversion from thinking about Mandy. For a while, anyway. He listened to the babble of voices, the insipid din of canned laughter, and tried to figure out where he and Mandy were going to take this thing.

If the diamonds were stolen, they'd have to be turned in. To whom? The FBI? Or was there some special jewel-smuggling board in charge of these things? He'd ask Moe to look into it for him.

If the diamonds *weren't* stolen, then they were Mandy's to keep. Except that if she kept them, she'd have two trigger-happy SOBs on her tail.

Two trigger-happy SOBs who happened to be in possession of Jack's doll. His doll full of diamonds. *His* diamonds.

Mandy was deeply asleep now, her rib cage rising and falling in an even rhythm. Jack was pretty wiped out himself. He forced himself to stay awake until the ten o'clock news came on. But there were no reports about missing gemstones, slashed tires, or gorgeous doll makers.

Jack snapped off the television and looked at Mandy. She was still sleeping on her side, her back to him. It was a wide bed; she'd left him more than enough room. He'd just lie down for a while.

And if sprawling out next to her body offered the utmost test of his willpower? If sharing a bed with Mandy Harlon was like unveiling a buffet within reach of a ravenous man?

He wasn't ravenous. He wasn't some overgrown adolescent with his brain in his pants. He was an adult, firmly in control of the situation.

So what if the most alluring woman he'd ever met was lying beside him on this nice, comfortable bed? So what if his nostrils filled with her clean, feminine scent? So what if one slight move would have her in his arms, his lips buried in her hair, his hands cupping her breasts?

He was almost too tired to care.

Almost.

Chapter Five

Her lips moved.

Half-asleep, she felt warmth against her mouth, tender pressure, a gentle invitation she welcomed with the mindless delight of someone who wasn't quite awake—and didn't want to be. If she woke up, she might start thinking. And if she started thinking, she would no doubt stop kissing him.

So she remained in that relaxed limbo between sleep and wakefulness and let herself respond to his kiss. She sighed as he teased her mouth with his, as he nipped her lower lip and caressed the corners of her smile with his lips. She sank into the lush sensation of his fingers stroking her hair back from her cheeks, his hands framing her face, his body rising slightly, urging her onto her back.

His mouth covered hers again, a little less gently, a little more persuasively. This was no longer an invitation. It was an outright seduction.

And she responded. A spasm of yearning seized her, deep in the cradle of her hips. Her eyelids flew open. She could no longer pretend to be dozing.

Her eyes rapidly adjusted to the dark. She stared up at Jack, at his chiseled features, his luminous brown eyes and his sensuous mouth. "What are you doing?" she whispered.

He smiled slightly. "You know damned well what I'm doing."

"Well, I'm not sure it's such a good idea."

His smile expanded into a husky laugh. "It's the best idea we've had so far."

"It's the *only* idea we've had. We were supposed to figure out what we were going to do—"

"Right now, we're going to do this," he said, twining his fingers through the tangled strands of hair at her temples and covering her mouth with his once more. His lips were strong and certain and honest.

She had to match his honesty. Only a hypocrite would pull away from a kiss they both wanted so much.

And really, they didn't have to go beyond a kiss. She could keep the situation under control.

Hesitantly, she lifted her hands to his shoulders. Through his shirt she felt an unyielding sculpture of bone and sinew. He rose higher, bracing himself with his forearms so that his chest hovered above hers. He grazed her cheeks, her forehead, the bridge of her nose, the dainty notch of her upper lip, and then he angled his head slightly and skimmed her lips with his tongue.

Whatever control she might have had evanesced, leaving in its place an emptiness that cried out to be filled. Her lips parted for him, and she dug her fingertips into the taut muscles of his back. Her tongue met his and they both groaned.

She had never wanted a kiss so desperately before. Never needed a kiss the way she needed this one. Never needed a man the way she needed Jack—suddenly, fiercely, implacably. Her arms tightened around him, pulling him fully onto her. He settled himself between her thighs, and she felt the hardness of him through his clothing and hers, felt his hunger in the slow, rhythmic surges of his hips against hers, in the plundering thrusts of his tongue, in the raggedness of his breath as his chest crushed her breasts.

Her hips rose off the mattress to meet him. His shudder of reaction aroused her even more.

Tearing his mouth from hers, he groaned again. His hands roamed deep into her hair, behind her ears, down to her shoulders. "Mandy," he murmured, his voice thick and unsteady. His knee rubbed against the inside of her thigh; one of his hands slid forward to skim her breast before he began to unbutton his own shirt.

She considered the wisdom of halting him now, before it was too late. She had already decided this wasn't supposed to go beyond a kiss. At least, her brain had decided.

Her heart seemed to be of another opinion. So did her hands, which moved, as if bewitched, to his shirt-front. As he undid another button and another, she shoved back the cotton broadcloth, slipped her hands inside and let them roam across his chest. His skin was hot, sleek. His muscles flexed against her palms; his nipples stiffened. His breath caught as she let her hands wander lower, across the taut surface of his stomach and down to the edge of his jeans.

Impatient, he yanked his shirt free from the waistband of his jeans, giving her more room, more freedom. His thumb hooked around the snap of his fly as he bent to kiss her again.

The telephone rang.

Jack held his breath for a moment, then let it out on a long, miserable sigh. The phone rang a second time, shrill and reproachful.

Mandy let her hands fall to the mattress. Pushing himself up to sit, he muttered a curse. His respiration was harsh and erratic. So was hers.

The phone rang a third time. "I reckon you ought to answer it," she said, commanding her fingers to stop wanting the feel of him.

He reached over her for the phone on the night table beside her. "Yeah?" he barked into the mouthpiece.

Through the receiver she heard a high-pitched babble. He listened for a moment, his face contorting into a scowl. "Hang on a second." He twisted to glance at Mandy. "Does Jessie have a wife named Iris?"

"An ex-wife," Mandy answered, her frown matching his. "Why?"

He turned back to the phone. "Yeah. When did it happen?" He listened some more. "How bad...? Uh-huh... Where are you now?" He listened. "She's here. Do you want to talk to her...? Okay. We'll be there as soon as we can."

He slammed down the phone, swung his legs off the bed and buttoned his shirt.

She watched him with building dread. Why had he questioned her about Iris? Why had he launched himself off the bed? Why was he stalking around the room like a caged tiger when he could be in her arms, holding her to him, telling her not to worry?

She worried. "What's going on?" she asked in a soft, tremulous voice.

"We've got to go back to Kentucky."

"Why?"

"Jessie's been hurt."

AT MIDNIGHT, the highway was nearly empty, a curving slick of black that cut through the rolling hills and glistened like patent leather from the day's rain. Mandy kept her eyes on the road, her hands white knuckled on the wheel.

Jack envied her for having the opportunity to drive. It gave her something to focus on; she had no room in her mind for what they were moving toward—or where they were coming from. Her grip on the wheel and the determined set of her jaw were more likely caused by anxiety about her brother than by frustration about what she and Jack hadn't been able to finish in the motel room.

Just thinking about it caused his own tension level to soar in a way that had nothing to do with Jessie's well-being.

Her lips. Her hair. Her tongue sparring with his, circling it, teasing and tantalizing. Her breasts, round and pliant, pressing up into his chest. Her soft, cool hands dancing across his skin, electrifying every nerve in his body. Her long legs shifting restlessly under him. The dark valley between her thighs, welcoming the rocking motion of his hips, moving to his sinuous tempo.

It was torture to think about, but he couldn't stop. He couldn't stop imagining what she'd look like naked, what those ripe breasts would taste like, what she would sound like when she cried out in ecstasy. He couldn't stop dreaming about the feel of her surrounding him, damp and eager, drawing him in, pulsing around him until they both exploded.

Definitely torture. He shifted his legs and forced himself to think only about Jessie.

At the end of a long road, Canaan Community Hospital stood in the glow of lights. Mandy found a parking space. Her face was pale, her lower lip caught between her teeth.

He wanted to suck on that lower lip himself—and on countless other parts of her anatomy. But he couldn't indulge in fantasies right now. Mandy needed him for support, for reassurance. "Your sister-in-law told me Jessie's going to be all right," he said, taking her arm as they started across the parking lot. "He just got a little roughed up."

"First of all," Mandy retorted grimly, "you don't get admitted to a hospital for being a little roughed up. Second of all, Iris isn't my sister-in-law."

"Your *ex*-sister-in-law."

"I don't even know why she's here with him. They've been legally divorced for two years, and whenever they talk it degenerates into World War Three."

"Do you think *she* roughed him up?"

"No," Mandy said, deflating with a sigh. "That's the worst part of it—guessing who did this to my brother. Lord help me, if those beasts so much as touched him..."

"Let's not jump to conclusions," Jack said in his most ameliorating voice, even though he'd already jumped to the same conclusion. "Look, maybe your brother was in a bar, having a few, and someone cast aspersions on his favorite baseball team or something."

"Sure," she snorted. "Those thugs almost killed you today. They shot at my truck. They ransacked my house. And you think my brother just happened to walk into someone's fist at a bar?"

"All I'm saying is, let's talk to him before we get more upset than we need to be."

"Here's a better idea," she snapped. "You don't have to be upset at all. I'll be upset for both of us, in just the right amount."

He let her sarcasm roll off him. In truth, he was as upset as she was. But someone had to keep calm. And maybe, just maybe, whatever had happened to Jessie was a mere coincidence.

Mandy stalked ahead of him, over to the visitors desk. By the time he reached her, she and the woman behind it were deep in conversation. "Yes, well his ex-wife said we need to talk to him," Mandy was saying.

"I'm sorry," the woman said. "We don't allow visitors past nine."

"Iris is still here." Mandy glanced questioningly at Jack, who shrugged. "She called us from here forty-five minutes ago and told us to come. If she's still here, I ought to be allowed to see him. She's not even his kin."

The woman behind the counter looked dubious. She turned and tapped the keyboard of her computer, entering information. Frowning slightly, she lifted a telephone and punched in a number.

"I see," she said, avoiding eye contact with Mandy. Jack craned his neck but was unable to read what was on the monitor. "I see. Now? Okay." She hung up and turned back to Mandy. "Your brother is still in the emergency room."

"Why? Iris said he'd been admitted."

"I believe they're holding him there so you can see him."

Mandy turned toward the hall the receptionist pointed to and headed off at a sprint. Jack raced after her. He nearly collided with an orderly pushing a cart of cleaning supplies, and Mandy pushed through a pair of swinging doors so sharply they swung back hard, nearly smacking him in the face. He hurried through them and glimpsed Mandy turning left at the end of the hall. Her hair caught the overhead fluorescent lights, waving behind her head like a flag of fire. He caught up to her just as she reached a door marked Emergency Room.

Mandy marched directly to the desk. "I'm looking for Jessie Harlon. Where is he?"

Without lowering the phone, the nurse gestured behind her. Mandy and Jack approached the small, curtained examining area.

Jack could scarcely see Jessie; his view was blocked by a thin woman clad entirely in black, her platinum hair shorn in a spiky, punk crew cut. "I'll tell you-all this, Mandy," the woman drawled when she saw Mandy, "someone oughtta have wired Jessie's jaw shut a long time ago. He's almost tolerable when he can't talk."

"Great seeing you, too, Iris," Mandy said none too graciously. She pushed past the woman in black and bowed over the bed. "Jessie, Jessie, what happened to you?"

Jessie grunted. An expressive grunt, Jack had to admit, but an unintelligible one.

Iris eyed Jack and offered a wry smile. "Finally, I don't have to listen to him mouthin' off at me. You want some more painkiller, Jessie?"

He grunted again, then spotted Jack and flickered his eyelids. More precisely, one eyelid. The other one was swollen and purple. And his right wrist was strapped into a molded plastic splint.

"Say something, Jessie," Jack requested.

Jessie bared his teeth, exposing enough metal wire to construct a suspension bridge. He grunted.

"They dislocated his jaw," Iris explained. "Doctor said it's got to be wired shut for a few days. The poor boy's gonna have to live by the straw. Now, I know I got the blender in the divorce settlement, but I intend to be really big about this and give it back to him. Matter of fact, seein' as he never got the hang of it, I reckon I'll have to be fixin' all his food for him during this convalescence."

Jessie grunted again.

"Who did this to you?" Mandy asked, sitting cautiously beside Jessie on the bed. "Those two thugs? Blink once for yes, twice for no."

Jessie blinked once. Twice. Three times.

Iris snorted. "Poor Jessie never quite got the hang of arithmetic." She slumped onto a folding metal chair near the bed and twirled her bangle bracelet, a thick silver monstrosity that resembled a snake devouring its tail. "What happened was, I had called Jessie to discuss a certain business matter with him—"

Jessie growled.

She sent him a look of annoyance. "I don't think it's such a big deal if you put my name back on your health insurance. No law says we gotta be married for that."

Jessie grunted. "I think some laws do stipulate that," Jack interjected helpfully.

"Well, jeez, Louise. I got this fantastic new job at Miss Nancy's Bridal Shop, but they don't include health insurance. I mean, what if *I'd* been the one to get bushwhacked, 'stead of him? The hospital would have given me a spool of wire and said, 'Sorry lady, you're on your own.'"

Miss Nancy's Bridal Shop? With her snake bracelet, silver skull earrings, knee-high black boots and black-enameled fingernails, Jack couldn't imagine her selling bridal gowns.

"Anyhow," she continued, "so I'm on the phone with Jessie, and he's jawin' at me, callin' me the usual, when suddenly his voice changes, like. He says, 'Iris, I got me some trouble. Call Bill McIntyre and tell him to get his butt over here.' Well, say what you will, Mandy, but I've always had a soft spot in my heart for Jessie here. Even when we were married."

I should hope so, Jack thought.

"So I tried to locate McIntyre. But nobody knew where he was. Well, I'm gettin' pretty worked up at this point, so I hopped on my bike and roared on over there. Found him beaten up some, his eye black and his jaw all swollen. His house was a mess, too. I wasn't gonna stick around and straighten up, though. I got him over to the hospital as quick as I could.''

"What have the doctors done for him?" Mandy asked.

"They checked him out, took lots of X rays and clicked their tongues. Seems he's got bruised ribs and a sprained wrist—along with the dislocated jaw."

"Did the thugs do this?" Mandy asked her brother.

Jessie blinked three times.

"Maybe he's saying yes and no," Jack suggested.

Jessie blinked once.

"One thug," Jack guessed.

Jessie blinked once.

Mandy let out a low sigh that sounded suspiciously like a sob. "This is all my fault."

"Oh, now, let's not start assigning blame," said Jack.

"What thug?" Iris asked. "Who are these guys, anyway?"

Jack's gaze met Mandy's. Her bag rested on her lap, and she closed her arms protectively around it. Only one thing seemed to have put it out of her mind, Jack recalled: making love. When he'd been kissing her, she'd been too busy hugging him to hug her precious bag with the jewels in it.

"Jessie, who are these thugs Mandy's talkin' about?"

Jessie grunted at his former wife.

Mandy continued to battle tears. Her lovely blue eyes glistened; her lower lip trembled. "Jessie, I'm so sorry—"

"We'd better go," Jack intervened, anxious to get her away before she either spilled the beans to Iris or fell apart completely. "Come on, Mandy. Let's let the hospital get Jessie into a room for the night."

She seemed to understand why he was urging her away from her brother. "All right," she complied, sniffling away a tear and rising from the bed. She bowed over Jessie and kissed his cheek. "You take care, now," she murmured. "I'll make sure the man who did this pays. I'll find Bill McIntyre and tell him to get the bastard behind bars, okay?"

Jessie blinked once, then reached out with his unsplinted left hand and gave Mandy's hand a squeeze.

"We'll get him," Jack vowed, tucking his hand around Mandy's arm.

"What thugs?" Iris called after them as they stepped through the break in the curtain.

Out in the waiting area, Mandy seemed to regain her courage. She drew her spine straight and shrugged out of Jack's protective hold. "I swear to God," she muttered through gritted teeth, "if I ever get my hands on that good-for-nothing lowlife—"

"That goes double for me," Jack concurred. He was relieved that her spirit had returned, but also a bit regretful. He saw little chance of her leaning on him when she was like this, all fired up and raring for a fight.

He admired her spunk—more than admired it. His life might depend on it. But how was he going to be her hero if she could fend for herself?

Hell, when did he start wanting to be a hero—hers or anyone else's? All he wanted was his Moe doll.

And maybe the rest of the night in bed with her.

They left the emergency room through a different door and found themselves outside, strolling down a driveway where a couple of ambulances were parked. The night air was cool and damp, refreshing after the overconditioned atmosphere inside the hospital. Jack took deep breaths, hoping to clear his head. The intensity of the day and the lateness of the hour were beginning to take their toll on him.

"If you'd like, we could find a closer motel to spend the night," he suggested, figuring Mandy wouldn't want to make the forty-five-minute drive back to Huntington. "Or we could chance returning to your house. How far are we from Harrow, anyway?"

"Your suitcase is still in Huntington."

"Big deal. I'll pick it up tomorrow."

She frowned thoughtfully. "I don't know if my house is safe. Those guys know where I live."

"Is there anywhere else in the area we could stay?" Jack asked as they circled around to the front of the building and headed toward Mandy's truck. "I know Harrow isn't renowned for its four-star hotels, but there must be a motel somewhere near the highway."

"Oh, Jack . . ." She sighed. "I *want* to go home. I want my house to be safe again."

"It will be, once we nail those hooligans. First thing tomorrow, we'll file assault charges on Jessie's behalf, and—"

He froze in midsentence. There, sitting on the back shelf of a car, propped up in the rear window, was his Moe doll.

He clamped his hand over Mandy's shoulder and pulled her to a halt. "Mandy," he whispered. "Is that what I think it is?"

She turned to look at what he was pointing at. He felt her flinch. "Oh, my God."

"I want my doll." He started toward the car.

She hauled him back. "If that's your Moe doll, then that's their car. Which means they're here."

What she said made sense—but he wasn't in the mood for sense. Something snapped inside him, unleashing his fury. Fury at the bastards who'd hurt her brother and threatened her. Fury at the fact that Jessie was lying in a flowered hospital gown with his jaw wired shut and his ex-wife yammering at him. Fury at the realization that Mandy's house was no longer safe. Fury at the violence that had torn her from his arms. Fury that Moe's doll was in that car instead of in his hands.

"I don't care," he muttered, breaking free of her and stalking across the lot. "I'm gonna get my doll. I want it. It's mine."

She remained where she was, watching him uncertainly. "Jack . . ."

He slowed his pace as he neared the car. He recognized it as the sedan that had run him off the road that afternoon. The tires he'd slashed had evidently been replaced, but the sides of the car were still splattered with mud.

A good ten feet from the car, he paused and knelt down to check underneath. No one was lying in wait there. He glanced around to the driver's side, then the passenger side. No one.

He took a few more steps, then he rose on tiptoe and peered into the car. Someone could be crouching on the floor, prepared to spring at him. This could be a trap. He had to be cautious.

He inched forward another step, and another.

"Jack!"

Mandy's scream cut through the night, shattering the air. He spun around in time to see her enveloped in a large shadow. A man-shaped shadow, restraining her in his arms, pinning her hands to her sides and pressing her back against him.

Shoving the barrel of a revolver under her chin.

Jack recognized the gun. The man. The voice, taut and menacing.

"Give me the diamonds or she dies."

Chapter Six

This man is going to kill me.

The dawning comprehension washed over her like an inky tidal wave, obliterating everything around her. And then the wave ebbed, leaving her with an almost too clear view of everything.

Her life. Her fate.

Jack.

His eyes reached to her across the distance, across one brief, endless fragment of time. Then the corners of his lips twitched, neither up nor down, just twitched, as if he would have spoken to her if he could.

The beast holding her jammed the gun more forcefully into her neck. His voice was surprisingly normal, given the circumstances. His accent was northern. She'd heard it hours earlier, at her house, through the floorboards of the kitchen. The sound of it made her stomach heave.

"Just give me the diamonds," he said.

Jack took a step toward them and directed his gaze to the man behind her. "What diamonds?" he asked.

"You know what diamonds."

"I do?" Jack scowled in sheer bewilderment at Mandy. An Oscar-caliber performance, she decided.

Her hand fisted against her purse, still dangling from her shoulder. If the thug opened it, she and Jack would undoubtedly pay the ultimate price for what he found inside.

"Don't play games with me," the man snarled as Jack took another step toward them.

"Play games?" His eyes widened in innocence. "What am I, an idiot? You think I'm going to play games with someone holding a gun to my woman's neck?"

My woman. The two words resonated inside her. She ought to be plotting her next move—or imploring God to leave the Pearly Gates open for her imminent arrival. But all she could think about was that Jack had called her his woman.

"Look, pal," he said to the thug, "if I knew what you were talking about, believe you me, I'd give you whatever you wanted."

"You know damned well what I'm talking about. You were going to break into my car."

"To get the doll. It's mine."

"You give me the diamonds, I'll give you the doll."

Jack's eyes glittered, and Mandy's spirits plummeted. She knew Jack wanted that doll, wanted it

passionately. Would he bargain away her diamonds—
and possibly her life—just to get his hands on it?

"I haven't got any diamonds to give you," he
swore.

"You're lying."

"I'm—" Abruptly he swung his head skyward and
gasped. "Whoa! Did you see that?"

The gunman looked up. Jack hurled himself forward, catching the guy in his midsection. A loud me-
tallic *clank* told her he'd dropped the gun.

Mandy fell to her knees and groped along the
ground in search of the gun. She could hear the sounds
of the scuffle behind her. She spotted the weapon on
the far side of Jack. Her purse, she discovered, had
somehow gotten kicked under a car.

She reached between the rear tires and retrieved the
purse. Then she walked slowly toward the gun, hoping not to catch the assailant's attention before she had
his weapon in her hand.

"Hey!" someone shouted from the hospital's entry. A beefy, uniformed security guard momentarily
blinded her with the beam of his swinging flashlight as
he loped across the parking lot. "What the heck is
going on out here?"

The man wriggled away from Jack, snatched the
gun and staggered to his car. Mandy knelt down beside Jack, who pulled himself up to sit with discour-
aging slowness. In the uneven light she couldn't tell
how badly he was hurt.

"Jack?" she whispered.

He was panting too hard to reply. However, he wrapped his arm sluggishly around her shoulders and pulled her to him. She leaned on him—and then realized he was leaning on her.

The guard reached them and squatted down. Mandy was vaguely aware of a car engine revving in the distance, but her attention was drawn by the guard's flashlight beam as he ran it over Jack's face. A thin thread of blood trickled from his lower lip, and one of his cheekbones looked suspiciously rosy.

"You-all want to tell me what happened?" the guard asked.

"He's getting away," Jack mumbled, then scowled and dug into his pocket. He pulled out a handkerchief and pressed it to his lower lip. "Why don't you go chase him?"

"Just tell me what happened. We'll catch up to that old boy later."

Mandy watched Jack carefully. If he told the truth, he'd have to divulge the existence of the diamonds in her purse, and she'd have to turn them over to this unknown rent-a-cop.

To rescue her, Jack had sacrificed his chance to get the Moe doll. She couldn't expect him to lie for her, too.

"He tried to hold us up," Jack said, his words muffled by the linen wadded against his lip. "He had a gun."

"I'm not a police officer," the guard explained. "But if you-all want to come inside, we can contact the police and file a report."

"No." Jack sighed. "It's not worth the time. It was just an attempted mugging."

"He comes from New York City," Mandy explained to the guard.

"Well, maybe you oughtta come on in, anyway, and have a medic look you over."

"No," Jack said, standing up. "I'm all right. Just a split lip." He smiled crookedly at the guard. "I still have my wallet, even."

The guard ran the flashlight up and down Mandy, who stood, as well. "Keep an eye out for yourselves, folks. Boy, it sure does bother me when that big-city crime starts filterin' down to us."

"We don't like it much in the big city, either," Jack muttered, his smile turning wry.

"Well, you-all take care of yourself. Put some ice on that lip, son," the guard said as he headed back to the hospital.

As soon as he was gone, Mandy expected Jack to slump back to the ground. He didn't, though. His eyes remained sharp as he surveyed the lot and sighed.

Around them rose the quiet sounds of night: a chorus of crickets serenading from the border of grass planted around the parking lot, a dark wind ruffling past her ears and into her hair, Jack's slow, labored breath, the thumping of her heart against her ribs.

She glanced at Jack. He returned her stare. She saw outrage in his eyes.

"Let's get in the truck," he said, his tone low and constrained.

"Okay." She tucked her hand around her purse and strode to the truck. Was Jack angry with her?

Oh, Lord—it *was* her fault. All of it. What had happened to Jessie, what had happened to Jack. All of it.

By the time they got into the truck, her vision was swimming again, this time through an ocean of tears. She covered her face with her hands and tried not to sob out loud.

When she peeked at Jack through her wet fingers, she saw that he was resting against the upholstery, his head rolled back and his eyes closed.

He seemed to sense her gaze on him, because he attempted a smile. "I'd give you my handkerchief to weep into, but it's got blood all over it."

She'd always prided herself on being strong, seldom given to tears. But not now. "I hate those diamonds," she moaned, flinging her purse onto the floor near Jack's feet. "I've got a brother with a dislocated jaw, and you're all beaten to a pulp—"

"Now wait a minute," Jack objected. "He lost that fight, not me. He's the pulp."

"Yes, but—"

"I mean, punch for punch, I had him cold. If that guard hadn't come along when he did, I would have knocked the sucker out."

Just like a man, she thought, her tears drying and her objectivity returning. "If that guard hadn't come along when he did, you and I might have wound up dead by gunshot."

"Not a chance," Jack boasted. "I was ahead on points, and I would have gotten the KO if—"

"Shut up, Jack."

He shot her a swift look. Her scowl inspired him to laugh. "Hey, you've got to take your fun where you find it."

She studied him in the spotty light. The bruise on his cheek was gaining definition, but his lip didn't look terribly swollen. "Are you all right? I mean . . ." Her gaze dropped to his chest.

"Wanna see?" he asked, tugging at the top button of his shirt.

"No," she said too quickly. As if the past hour hadn't occurred at all, she found herself remembering that beautiful chest of his, the sleek feel of it, the racing of his heart against her palm as she touched him, as she caressed him, as she dreamed of his hands touching her, caressing her. . . .

Jack had a remarkable way of muddling her brain, but right now she couldn't afford to be muddled. "What should we do?" she asked, deliberately staring at the spotlit sign above the hospital entry.

"Get some sleep," he said. "It's almost one o'clock."

"I've got to get rid of those diamonds."

"Huh?" He sat up straighter.

"I'm not kidding, Jack. Tomorrow morning I'm going to turn the damned diamonds over to the authorities."

"What authorities? That oaf McIntyre?"

"No. I'll call Bobby Lee and ask him for ideas."

"Your old boyfriend," Jack guessed. "You're going to give *him* the diamonds? Lady, if you're all that eager to get rid of them, I'll take them off your hands for you."

As attracted to Jack as she was, as aroused as she could become merely by thinking of him, as guilty as she felt about the punishment he'd endured thanks to her queer luck, she didn't doubt for a minute that he would be more than happy to take her diamonds off her hands.

Sure, he'd kissed her divinely. Sure, he'd passed up the opportunity to repossess his doll to save her from the thug. But the bottom line was, no matter what he felt for her, he wanted her diamonds.

Not that she could blame him. She wanted them, too.

"I reckon you're right," she conceded coolly. "We should get some sleep. I know a place we can spend the night," she said, turning on the engine and shifting into gear. "It's not far, and no one will ever find us there."

"It sounds perfect."

"It's not," she warned him, steering out of the parking lot.

"What's wrong with it?"

"Well, it doesn't have a bed."

"Mandy! I need a bed. I've just been in a fight."

"Which you claim to have won," she taunted, navigating the dark, damp roads.

"Even so... I'm a little sore."

"Don't worry. There are cushions."

"Where the hell are you taking me?"

Her only answer was a smile. Let him stew about it, she thought. Any man who could send her emotions on such a roller-coaster ride deserved something to worry about, even if it was only the sleeping provisions.

His worry increased as she cruised into the foothills, heading south toward Harrow. She knew these dark, serpentine roads well. Her headlights offered all the illumination she needed. That Jack felt it necessary to brace himself against the dashboard was a reflection of his city-slicker background.

They coasted through the heart of Harrow, passing the dark shops, the empty parking spaces, the tranquillity of a sleeping hamlet. Then they proceeded deeper into the woods, into the hills.

"Where are you taking me?" Jack asked once more, sounding less irritated than resigned.

"Someplace safe."

"And comfortable?"

"Comfortable enough."

"We're in the middle of nowhere."

"We're in Harrow, Kentucky."

"I rest my case."

"I wish to high heaven you would."

His hands tightened on the dashboard. "We're not on the road anymore."

The truck bumped over a dead tree limb that lay in its path. "Not a paved road."

"Cripes. Is this the dirt road I drove off this afternoon?"

"Probably not. There's I don't know how many dirt roads in the area."

He issued a low, heartfelt prayer. "I really want to live, Mandy. Okay? No joke. Don't drive me over a cliff."

"Treat me right and I won't."

The road twisted and curved, but she knew its idiosyncrasies. She'd been driving this particular dirt road since long before she'd been legally old enough to drive at all. Grampa Harlon used to perch her on his lap and let her steer while he worked the floor pedals of his old Ford flatbed with the rebuilt engine.

"That's it," Jack murmured as the headlights illuminated a barn looming through the trees ahead. "I swear I drove past that barn this afternoon."

"You couldn't have. You were higher in the hills. These mountains are filled with old barns and dirt roads, Jack. And you probably believe all barns and dirt roads look alike."

"They do if you're from Manhattan," he agreed.

Reaching the barn, she shifted into neutral, climbed out and unlocked the padlock holding the doors shut.

She swung them both wide, then climbed back into the truck and drove slowly into the barn.

Jack gazed around him, looking perplexed. There was nothing so puzzling about the barn, as far as she knew. Gramma Harlon had cleared all the incriminating evidence out years ago.

"What is this place?" Jack asked as she shut off the engine.

"It's my hideaway." She reached for her purse, and he chivalrously handed it to her. "My Grampa Harlon used to run a still here."

"A still? As in moonshine?"

"Don't look so shocked, Jack. It wasn't like he was a bootlegger or anything. He just brewed some sour mash whiskey for the local trade. A lot better quality than anything you could buy in stores, from what I hear."

"You never drank it?"

She shook her head and got out of the truck. Jack met her at the tailgate and helped her draw the barn doors shut. She locked them from inside, blocking out what little moonlight they had.

She knew her way around the barn in the dark, though. In no time, she'd reached the shelf where she kept a kerosene lamp. She lit it and shook out the match. "My grampa, rest his soul, died when I was seventeen. Too young to have become much of a drinker. My gramma unloaded the still on a friend down in Hazard County. When she died, she left me this barn as well as the house. It's my hideaway."

"What do you use it to hide from?"

"Besides gunmen?" She shrugged. "I don't know. Sometimes it's just nice to get away from the house and listen to the trees. I *do* have cushions up in the loft. We'll be able to get some rest."

She moved around the truck to the ladder that led up to the loft, then glanced over her shoulder to make sure Jack was with her. He was less than a foot behind her. The golden lamplight spilled across his face, illuminating not just his bruised cheek but his dark, deep-set eyes, his disheveled hair, the quizzical twist of his lips.

Turning back, she swallowed and started up the ladder. "Watch your step," she said, wondering how many ways he would interpret the warning.

The ladder trembled under her as he planted his foot on the lowest rung, and then the next, and the next. In the loft, she set down the lamp and began gathering the oversize cushions she'd brought to the loft when she'd decided to turn it into a retreat. The light shifted behind her, and she turned to find Jack holding the lamp high and studying the wall across the loft.

"You've got posters hanging here."

"Do I really?" she said with pretended surprise. "Imagine that."

He scrutinized one of the posters, which she'd bought at a jazz festival in Atlanta a few years ago. "You really do like jazz, don't you?"

"I like all kinds of music." She sat on one of the cushions and pulled off her shoes. "Right now I'd like a lullaby, but I reckon I don't really need one. Blow out the lamp when you're done inspecting the premises."

She stretched out and let the plush, feather-stuffed pillows absorb her weary body. Through her lowered lids she detected the approaching light as Jack carried the lamp to her part of the loft. She squeezed her eyes more tightly shut, but that only magnified the sounds of him removing his shoes and his jacket, rearranging his cushions and sinking into them. She heard a squeak as he turned the screw that lowered the wick, and then the barn fell into darkness.

She let out a long breath. She should have fallen right to sleep, but she was too keyed up. Wind whistled through the trees outside the barn. An owl hooted far away.

She thought about Jessie's jaw. About Jack's lip. About a gun shoved up against her throat.

An involuntary shudder overtook her. She heard herself whimper.

Somehow, suddenly, Jack's arms were around her. She took refuge in them, in their marvelous warmth and strength. She could be fearless tomorrow. Tonight, when she'd felt her own death closing in on her, when two men near and dear to her had borne the injuries that should have been hers . . .

"Oh, God, Jack—I'm scared," she whispered. "I know I shouldn't be, but—"

"Why shouldn't you be?" He rubbed the taut muscles at the back of her neck, kneading out the tension.

"They're only diamonds, Jack. It's only a doll. We could have been killed."

"But we weren't." She burrowed into the shelter of his body, pressing her face against his shoulder and shamelessly accepting his comfort. "We weren't killed," he murmured in a low, soothing voice. "We're here, we're safe, and those jerks aren't going to get us."

In spite of the heat emanating from his body, she shivered uncontrollably. "I've never been this scared in my life."

"I have."

"You have?" She wondered what could be scarier than having a gun pointed at you.

"When I was a kid," he said quietly. "I had to fight for my life. First with my father and then on the streets, till Moe took me in." His hands moved up and down her back in a consoling pattern. "But I survived. I'm a survivor, Mandy. And so are you."

She leaned back and peered at him, the outlines of his face gradually becoming visible as her eyes adjusted to the dark. "Am I?"

He brought one hand forward to cup her face. His thumb slid gently over her cheek, wiping away a tear. "I wouldn't want you so much if you weren't," he answered, then leaned toward her and brushed his lips over hers.

The diamonds, she thought. The doll. The hospital. The gun.

None of it mattered, not now. All that mattered was surviving, generating new strength, courage, wisdom. Hope. All that mattered was this man who had saved her life, who had more faith in her than she had in herself.

She thought about his refusal to go after his precious doll when she'd been in trouble. She thought about how, any step of the way, he could have abandoned her, gone home to New York and left her to the terrifying mercies of the maniacs chasing her.

But he'd stayed. For her.

Her mouth opened to him. Her tongue tasted the salt of blood on his injured lip and she started to withdraw, but he pressed her down into the cushions and deepened the kiss, drinking her in, nibbling and sucking and devouring her as if he was as desperate for her as she was for him. Maybe he was.

She combed her fingers through his hair, behind his ears, down to his shoulders and around to the nape of his neck. He pulled his lips from hers and kissed her chin, the angular line of her jaw, the soft underside of it where the thug had pressed the gun barrel. He pressed his lips to the very same place, reclaiming it for her, healing it.

"Mandy," he whispered. "Amanda..." And his lips moved lower, following in the wake of his hands as they journeyed down the front of her blouse, undoing the buttons. He skimmed his fingers across the satin of her brassiere and she tried to lift herself up so he could reach the clasp. But his touch ignited her, sending all her strength downward to her hips where it pooled, liquid and hot, like lava.

He stroked her breasts until they strained at the glossy pink fabric, until her nipples were hard, protruding against the cloth. He bowed and covered one with his mouth, his hot breath filtering through the satin, making her half mad to feel his mouth against her skin.

She forced herself to sit up. He sat, too, straddling her lap, shoving her shirt down her arms and reaching behind her to undo the clasp.

She felt for his shirt buttons with trembling fingers. Instead of helping her to undress him, he closed his hands over her breasts, massaging them, circling them with his palms and tugging at her swollen nipples. Sandwiched between his knees, her hips writhed as she sank helplessly back into the cushions.

He did her the kindness of removing his shirt. Then he bent to kiss one of her breasts and the other, and then the hollow between them. She stroked his back, the warm smooth skin she'd admired in the motel room a lifetime ago. She explored the curve of his rib cage, the taut surface of his stomach, the narrow indentation of his navel. He groaned against her skin, and groaned again when she moved her hands to his hips and around to caress the streamlined muscles of his buttocks.

He murmured something—a curse, a plea, she wasn't sure. And then his hands were on her jeans, manipulating the button, yanking on the zipper, shoving the denim down her legs. He hastily disposed of his own jeans as well, and descended into her arms.

She wove her legs through his, feeling him hard and seeking against her belly, feeling his thigh flex against her and make her arch to him. He brought his hand down to her bottom, digging his fingers into the rounded flesh and pressing her even more tightly to him. She heard herself gasp as the heat and dampness increased inside her, building in urgency, threatening to break through and flood her soul.

He brought his hand forward, around her thigh and into the dense thatch of curls between her legs. He moved his thumb over her inflamed flesh and slid his fingers deep. Her breath caught in her throat as she arched again, needing, needing so much.

Jack. She needed Jack.

She reached down and took him in her hands. He was already fully aroused, and when she skimmed her fingers the length of him, he groaned and pulsed hot against her palms. He let her lead him, let her spread her legs around him and guide him until his hardness met her softness.

He thrust inside her, and she was no longer leading. He was the power, carrying her, driving her onward. Each fierce surge of his body fed the growing pressure within her. Each lunge gave more, took more, exposed more of her to the sweet, sharp pleasure of her response.

It had never been like this before. She'd never felt so revealed, so utterly naked, so open to a man's love. She clung to his shoulders as if hanging on for dear life—and for a moment, a crazed, precarious instant, she truly believed she was closer to death in his arms than she'd been when that beast had aimed his gun at her. If Jack made her feel anything more wonderful than what she was already feeling, she would surely die.

And then it erupted into something much more wonderful. Exquisite spasms of bliss wrenched her, throbbed through her, conquered her body and her mind, her heart and her soul.

She felt more alive than ever. Jack had saved her life, and now he had given her himself.

He had given her *herself*.

Her customers believed rose-quartz crystals could make dreams come true. But as Mandy buried her lips against his shoulder and moaned in complete, joyful surrender, she believed only in Jack Slater.

Chapter Seven

His first impression, once she'd shut off the truck engine, was that this remote, rickety barn in the woods was too quiet. He could hear the timber creaking, nocturnal animals pawing the ground outside the barn, the eerie hush of a forest in repose.

But then, bless her, Mandy had broken that silence.

With a sob.

He'd felt privileged to gather her into his arms, honored that she would let him see her fear. When that homicidal brute had his gun pointed at her, she hadn't revealed the merest glimmer of panic. She'd remained composed, and had the presence of mind to go after the guy's gun.

Jack knew she would have used that gun, too, if she'd had to. He had seen her wielding her shotgun. He didn't doubt that she could shoot—probably better than he could.

But when she'd let out that small, tormented cry in the smothering soundlessness of her grandfather's old barn, Jack had understood how much he'd really wanted to save her. So much, he'd been willing to risk getting himself shot. He would gladly have traded his life for hers.

Now, as he lay with her in the peaceful aftermath of their lovemaking, he knew why. At last he'd heard what he'd been longing to hear ever since he'd first laid eyes on her: a cry not of grief or fear but of rapture as her sultry body undulated around him, drawing from him a pleasure so excruciating he'd all but cried out himself.

He wove his fingers through her hair, amazed at how something so soft and silky could be so thick. The coppery tendrils twined around his hand, capturing him in their alluring web. He wanted her the way Moe wanted his doll—because she gave him hope. Because she made his life better.

"So," he said, caressing the skin behind her earlobe and smiling when she let out a throaty purring sound. "You're all through with this Bobby Lee person, aren't you?"

Her eyes widened in surprise. He wondered whether he'd said something wrong.

"Bobby Lee and I are friends."

"Are you lovers?"

"I hardly think that's your business."

"Actually—" he skimmed his hand the length of her body, rising over her breasts, swooping down at her waist and across the slight curve of her belly until he reached the warmth between her legs "—I think it *is* my business."

"Jack..." Her voice dissolved into another moan. "Don't do that. I can't think."

He pulled his hand away slowly, deliberately rubbing against her. "I sure as hell don't want to keep you from thinking. Tell me about him."

"Why don't you tell me about your girlfriends in New York?"

He shrugged. "There's nothing to tell. I go out, I have dates, but there's been nobody special for a long time." Until now, he almost added. But she'd already had enough scares for one night. They'd bared their bodies. They could bare their souls once things settled down.

"I reckon there must be millions of beautiful women in New York City," she said.

"I reckon there must be," he mimicked her drawl. "So what?"

"So, why are you wasting time with me?" Her eyes glinted, cool and pale in the shadows. "I don't suppose it has anything to do with my diamonds, does it?"

He could have been offended. He chose to laugh instead. "Wait a minute. Here I am with the sexiest, sassiest, most sensational woman I've ever met, and we've just shared something about as powerful as Hurricane Andrew—only a whole lot more fun—and you think I give a damn about a bag of crystalized carbon?"

"Yes."

"Well, you're wrong."

"You want your doll. That's the only reason you're still here."

It wasn't an accusation, not really. Simply a statement of the truth—or, more accurately, her take on the truth.

"Do you know what I like best about that doll?" he asked.

"It's full of diamonds."

"Wrong."

"You think it's going to cure Moe Kaplan's arthritis."

"*You* made it. That's the best thing about it. *You* made it."

He felt her gaze on him, studying him as if she was trying to decide whether to believe him. He thought it might speed things along if he kissed her, so he did.

At first she didn't react. But before long her lips were moving with his, her breath blending with his, her hands sliding along his back, her body surging and her soft sigh of passion singing through the air. If she was going to kiss him like this, he didn't care what she thought. All that mattered was her response to him, the velvet texture of her skin against his, the taunting forays of her tongue into his mouth, her fingernails scraping the skin along his spine.

This was all he needed to know: she wanted him as much as he wanted her.

With a ragged gasp, he drew back. What if she *didn't* want him as much as he wanted her? What if she was still somehow involved with Bobby Lee?

"It's your turn," he murmured, tracing her lower lip with his index finger.

"My turn?" Her voice was thick, her eyes unfocused.

"Tell me about Bobby Lee."

She cleared her throat. Her focus sharpened. "I'm chilly. Do you mind if I get a blanket?"

"Be my guest." Now that his sweat had dried and his pulse rate had returned to near normal, he wasn't quite so warm, either. Mandy's stalling tactics lowered his thermostat even more.

She padded barefoot across the loft, vanishing into the shadows. When she returned, she was carrying a thick woolen quilt, which she shook out and spread over Jack and the cushions. She wriggled under the blanket's cozy folds. He closed his arms possessively around her and waited for her to speak.

"He's a good friend," she said.

"How good?"

Through the shadows he could see her canny smile. "You're jealous, aren't you?"

"Getting jealouser by the minute. Why won't you tell me about him?"

"Because it's over—except for the friendship."

"What was it before it was over?"

"Well . . . we lived together for two years."

"Okay." And really, it was. Now that he'd found out the worst, he could accept it. "Was he from Harrow?"

She chuckled. "Bobby Lee Nash? Heavens, no. He was from Atlanta. The great-great-great-grandson of a colonel in the Confederate Army. Where do you think the name Bobby Lee came from?"

"Robert E. Lee?" Jack guessed.

"The one and only. The Nashes are a very proper, very rich, very Atlanta family. And Bobby Lee is a very proper, very rich, very Atlanta lawyer."

Jack folded his hand around hers to let her know that his questions reflected interest, not any misplaced rivalry. "How did you meet him?"

She wove her fingers through his and stroked her thumb along his wrist, managing to turn him on as thoroughly as if her thumb were stroking somewhere else. "I'd gone to Atlanta for college. My mama thought it would be good for me to go to the big city and improve myself."

"You don't need any improvements," Jack pointed out.

Mandy laughed out loud. "I'm not so sure about that. In any case, what with my holding down part-time jobs and hanging out at night spots, college didn't improve me one whit. I wound up dropping out. I couldn't see spending all those thousands of dollars in tuition if I wasn't going to knuckle down and study. And as it turned out, I wasn't."

"Night spots?"

"Jazz clubs, rock clubs, midnight movies." She nestled closer to him, using his upper arm for a pillow. "I got a job as a secretary in a big law firm. Bobby Lee worked there."

"An office romance? Shame on you!"

"Oh, no—he was quite the gentleman about it. I told him I wouldn't sleep with someone I worked for, so he found me a job with one of his old law school buddies. It was a much smaller firm, upstairs in a musty old building, but they were involved in exciting work. Civil-rights cases. They let me help out with the research sometimes."

"And you got to move in with Bobby Lee."

"There was that," she confirmed, grinning slyly. "I reckon I did get an education of sorts while I was in Atlanta. Downstairs from the law office where I worked was a shop that sold all kinds of New Age materials. The women who ran it claimed to be witches—good ones, they said. White witches. They taught me lots of stuff about crystals."

"Rose-quartz crystals."

"That's right."

"What did the great-great-great-grandson think about that?"

"He thought they were nuttier than a pound of pralines." She shrugged. "Sometimes I reckon he thought I was nutty, too. But we got along well. We even talked about marriage, although the Nashes would have had a conniption if we'd ever gone through with it. They thought I was trash."

"What do you expect? They're descended from slave owners. They're obviously misguided."

Mandy chuckled. "Well, we never had to discuss marriage plans with his family. Gramma Harlon had a stroke—the first of several, as it turned out. My parents were living in Arizona by then, and Jessie and Iris were having lots of problems in their marriage, so I came back to Harrow to take care of her."

"And?"

She shrugged again. "Bobby Lee thought I shouldn't have."

"Shouldn't have what? Taken care of your grandmother?"

"Left Atlanta. Left him."

Jack scowled. Bobby Lee sounded like a bigger fool than his aristocratic parents. "I can't think of a better reason to leave Atlanta."

Mandy didn't speak for a minute. Her eyes shimmered with tears. Apparently, reminiscing about her grandmother made her maudlin.

"You understand," she whispered, and he realized her tears arose from something more complex. "Bobby Lee never did. It made no sense to him that I'd want to go back to the sticks, where there weren't any jazz clubs and concert halls—and there wasn't any Bobby Lee. To him, Harrow was nowhere. The end of the road. A hole in the ground. He just couldn't understand why I would consider my grandmother so important." She sighed, and the laugh that escaped her sounded melancholy. "Of course you would understand. Look at what you're going through for Moe Kaplan. You understand these things.''

Yes, he understood. He knew how it felt to be mistreated and, thanks to Moe, he knew how it felt to be loved. He'd learned to forgive his father, if not to forget. But he'd also learned what it meant to make a commitment to someone, to create a bond and accept all the responsibilities that came with love.

If Mandy's old flame couldn't comprehend something so basic, so essential to Mandy, he must not have known Mandy at all.

She curved her arm around Jack and pulled him down to her. He felt hunger in her kiss; he tasted tears on her lips. At least he knew they weren't tears of dread and despair. They were an honest, heartfelt expression of how she felt. And the snug embrace of her arms around his waist was another expression, and the eagerness of her tongue playing over his, and the bending of her leg between his, the seductive flexing of it.

He rolled onto his back, bringing her with him. Her long, firm body draped over him and he savored the weight of her. She was solid and healthy, not like the gaunt, fragile, fashionably emaciated women who seemed to populate his social circles in New York. When Mandy lay on top of him, he knew she was there, and he liked it.

She slithered down to kiss his chest, and he liked it even more. Her lips moved tentatively down his sternum and then across to lick one nipple and the other.

The friction of her tongue on his skin sent bolts of sensation searing down to his groin. He groaned in discomfort, in excitement.

He slid his hands up her sides and under her arms, and when she lifted herself off him, he moved forward to fondle her breasts.

She arched her back, and it was with both reluctance and impatience that he abandoned her breasts for her belly, and that for the hot cleft between her legs. Her breath grew short as he opened her and readied her, and she pressed her lips to the hollow of his shoulder and moaned against his skin, moaned as he brought her closer and closer. When she began to rock her hips in silent beseechment, he cupped his hands around her hips and pulled her down, sliding hard into her.

Her body shook as the force of her climax seized her. It had happened too fast; he hadn't even started to move. Yet the way she surged and contracted around him made him wild with pleasure.

He kept his hands tight on her hips, holding her still as he pushed deeper, as he plunged into the darkness of her again and again. Denying himself his own release was a kind of agony, but as he felt her relaxing, joining him for the journey, he knew the wait would be worth it. She propped herself up on her arms and smiled down at him, breaking free of his clasp and moving her hips on her own, pressing, shifting, twisting, sheathing him in her womanly warmth.

He brought one hand forward until his fingers found her warmth. His touch seemed to galvanize her. She closed her eyes and gasped, and he touched her again, and she was gone, soaring into heaven. This time he went with her.

A long time later he returned to earth, to the feather-filled pillows under him and the weary woman above him. Her arms lay languidly around his shoulders, around him, and when she sighed, her breath danced across his chest.

"We're good together, Mandy," he said. A gross understatement, but he wasn't sure what else he should say.

"Mmm." She sighed again. Maybe it was a yawn.

"Are you falling asleep?"

"Mmm."

She'd already fallen. Which meant he could say whatever he wanted. That they were better than good together—they were phenomenal. That he would do whatever it took to be her hero: fight the bad guys, protect her diamonds, escort her to all the night spots, raise capital so she could build a doll-making factory and buy her own rose-quartz mine in Brazil, if that was what she wanted. That he would storm Atlanta like General Sherman, and tell old Robert E. Lee Nash that letting Mandy slip out of his life proved he had grits where he should have had brains—and that Jack was eternally grateful to him.

He could tell her that even the mournful silence of this barn and these woods couldn't get to him. Not when he had her in his arms.

"WHERE'S YOUR SUPPLIER from?"

"Huh?" Mandy tried to open her eyes, but her lids resisted. She tunneled deeper under the quilt, where the air was warm and dark, and clung desperately to the last shreds of sleep.

Jack willfully tugged those shreds away. "Listen, Mandy—I've been thinking. Where's your supplier from?"

She groaned and peeked through her lashes. The barn was dappled with beams of morning light that seeped through the cracks and gaps between the wall planks. Next to her, Jack lay on his side, propped up on one elbow. His brown eyes were animated, his smile contagious.

She closed her eyes again. "Go back to sleep," she grumbled, trying to pull him back down under the blanket with her.

"It's morning," he said unnecessarily. "Wake up. We've got to make some plans."

"Plans?" She opened her eyes once more. They filled with the wondrous sight of him. One of her hands lay draped over his hip, the other molded to his chest. Remembering all the amazing things his body had made her feel last night, she wanted even more to pretend morning hadn't come.

"Where's your new quartz-crystal supplier from?" he asked yet again.

"New York City. Just like the old one."

"Perfect," he said, his eyes growing even brighter.

She found his rise-and-shine perkiness irritating. "What time is it?"

He shifted to read his watch. "Seven forty-five." Overriding her curse, he continued. "Here's the plan. We'll go after the supplier."

She really owed it to herself to pay attention. "What do you mean?"

"We'll go to New York and confront him."

"Right. Let me compose my last will and testament first."

"You think he'll try to nail us? No problem," Jack assured her. "We'll line up a bodyguard."

"What?"

"A bodyguard. A big, scary guy with a gun."

"I've had my fill of scary guys with guns, thank you."

"No, listen, Mandy. We've got to go after the supplier. That's the only way I'll ever get my doll back. The thugs are going to bring it to him."

"What makes you so sure of that?"

"It's stuffed with diamonds, isn't it?"

She sighed. Part of her agreed that his hypothesis made sense. Another part worried that, now that he'd spent a few divine hours satisfying his libido with her, he'd reverted to his number-one concern: the doll.

Don't think that way, she cautioned herself. *Don't think he cares more about the doll than about you.*

"I bet it would work," he was saying. "We'll hire ourselves an armed escort, track down the supplier and threaten the hell out of him. You'll bring your contract and your cancelled checks to prove you own the carton that was shipped to you. I'll bring my order form from Dido to prove I own the doll. We'll tell him to turn the doll over and leave you alone or we'll go to the authorities. He's the smuggler, not us. He's the one who's got something to hide."

"He also has his own militia." She sighed and closed her eyes, not to resume sleeping but because looking at Jack had a way of scrambling her brain. Seeing him filled her with memories of the way his lips had felt on her last night, and his hands, and his hard, male flesh invading her, doing sublime, intimate things to her.... Seeing him caused her to ponder such dangerous notions as love and devotion and forever.

Dear God. She'd gone and fallen in love with Jack Slater.

And all he could think about was getting his stupid doll back.

"Jack." She kept her voice low so he wouldn't hear the quiver in it. "Jack, I can't go to New York City with you."

"Why not? I think it would be more effective if we went together. It would show the guy we're not afraid of him, and we're not going to let him or his henchmen push us around. I think that's our best bet. We'll go, we'll intimidate him, and he'll turn over my doll. Really, Mandy, I can't imagine him giving me back the doll if I face off with him alone.''

A salty lump filled her throat and she swallowed it back down. If only he'd said, ''Come to New York with me because I love you, because I can't bear to be without you…'' But he hadn't. All he cared about was the diamonds.

''I can't go with you. I don't want to leave Jessie,'' she mumbled, grabbing the first excuse that entered her mind. A good excuse, too. Her brother was in the hospital because of her. Adding insult to injury, he was being harangued by Iris and couldn't talk back. Mandy couldn't leave him when he was so defenseless.

''Oh. Well. I see what you mean,'' Jack agreed. ''I suppose I'll have to go without you, then.'' Not, ''The hell with Jessie—I need you more than he does.'' Not, ''I'll stay here with you until he's better.''

I'll have to go without you.

The golden sunbeams sifting into the barn mocked her. She felt gloomy, miserable, more desolate now than she had with a gun jammed into her neck. Jack was going to leave her.

And she loved him.

Well, she'd damned well better stop loving him, she thought, snaking a hand out from under the blanket and grabbing her clothes. If Jack had an opinion about her getting dressed, he didn't verbalize it. She avoided looking at him, and eventually he rolled out from under the blanket and put on his own clothes.

When at last she glanced his way, he was tucking his shirt into his jeans and gazing about the barn. There wasn't much to see; the barn didn't hold much.

Except for memories. Too many recent, inflammatory memories. Mandy wondered whether she would ever feel comfortable there again.

"You don't have a coffeemaker here, do you?" he asked.

"Of course not," she snapped. "I haven't even got electricity."

"I guess we should head into town. I'm starving."

Great. His mind could in fact accommodate two distinct concepts: getting his doll, and putting food in his stomach.

How had she misread him so badly? How had she trusted him? He had seemed so able to understand her, and she had assumed they were communicating on some deeper level. She'd believed they were truly making love, not just having sex.

If she hadn't believed that, she would never have given so much of herself. She would never have responded so profoundly.

Maybe, as Jessie had warned her, she'd been out of circulation too long.

"So, what do you say?" Jack asked. He seemed to be in an astonishingly upbeat mood. "Let's go grab a bite down at the Sunnyside Café."

Oh, sure, she almost retorted. Let's be charming and friendly and pretend last night never happened.

A faint sound in the distance stopped her from letting loose with her sarcasm. She touched her index finger to her lips to silence him, then inclined her head and concentrated.

A car engine. Had the thugs found them?

Jack appeared to have heard the sound, as well. "Did you bring your rifle?" he asked.

"It's a shotgun," she muttered, just for the petty pleasure of contradicting him. She'd stashed the shotgun under the seat of her truck after fleeing from her house yesterday afternoon. She hadn't removed it, so it must still be there.

The car was drawing nearer. She hurried down the ladder, Jack right behind her, and pulled the shotgun out of the truck. By the time she had the trigger cocked, the car sounded to be close outside the barn. The engine chugged loudly, then died.

Jack pressed himself against the locked doors and angled his head toward the truck, indicating that she should hide behind it. She kept the shotgun perched on her shoulder, ready to use it if she had to. She'd already had her spirit demolished. She wasn't going to let anyone do damage to her body without putting up a serious fight.

From outside came a loud pounding on the door. "I know you're in there, Miss Amanda," Bill McIntyre bellowed. "You've got the doors locked from inside. I know you're in there."

"Bill," she groaned, lowering the shotgun and walking to the door.

"Don't let him in," Jack whispered. "He might arrest me again."

And if he does, don't count on me to get you released, she thought churlishly. Aloud she said, "At this point, we could surely use the protection of the law." She unlocked the padlock, pulled it out of the metal ring and eased open the doors.

Bill McIntyre stood on the other side, his four-wheel drive behind him and a sorry tale of dissipation written across his face. His eyes were puffy and bloodshot, his pudgy jaw unshaven, his shirt wrinkled.

"What nightmare did you escape from?" she asked.

"Don't shout," Bill pleaded, pressing his fingertips to his temples and wincing.

Mandy hadn't thought she was shouting. "Are you hung over?" she asked in a quieter voice.

"Lordy, I'm hanging so far over, one misstep and I'll be flat on my face." He gazed into the barn. "Nobody made a finer likker than your granddad, Mandy," he recollected, his tone laced with nostalgia. "Stuff I was drinkin' last night could take the tar off a breakdown lane." His eyes struggled for focus as he gave her the once-over. "How are you?"

Mandy risked a quick glance in Jack's direction. Physically she was all right. Emotionally she might require an autopsy. "I'm fine," she said.

"Mandy, I've come to apologize," Bill said, then turned to Jack. "My apologies to you, too, Mr. Slater.

It appears I was bamboozled by those two con artists whose tires you slashed."

"I never admitted to slashing them," Jack reminded him. "And I wasn't formally charged—"

"Lower your voice, son. I can hear you just fine." Bill cringed again, then shook his head dolefully. "Yessir, I was bamboozled. Emphasis on the middle syllable."

"They boozed you?"

"Tanked me up but good. Just one of them. I'm a mere man, you know. Somebody offers to take me out for a few drinks, hell, what man would say no?"

"An officer of the law might," she scolded. "You're not supposed to accept gifts from folks."

"It wasn't a gift. Just a couple of rounds of whiskey." He shook his head again. "More'n a couple, I reckon. And that weren't no whiskey like any I'd ever drunk before. I woke up in the back seat of the Bronco—" he jabbed his thumb toward the vehicle behind him "—and spent a good half hour searching the front seat for my head. This is not gonna be an easy day for me."

"It shouldn't be." Mandy lit into him, no longer bothering to speak softly. If she couldn't vent her anger at Jack, she damned well could vent it at Bill McIntyre. "While you were busy getting tanked, my brother was being assaulted by the other thug."

"I know, Mandy, I know. Lord knows I'm sorry. Iris gave me what-for, and I've sent him some flowers."

"Gee. That'll really help him."

"Hell, Iris is taking care of him better'n she ever did when they were married. She said she's bringing him back to her house, and she's gonna make homemade soup and spoon-feed him till they take the wire cutters to his jaw."

Maybe some good would come of all this, after all, Mandy thought wryly. Maybe Iris and Jessie would remember how to treat each other with kindness. Maybe someone's heart would heal.

"Did you check his house?" Jack spoke up. Just the husky, sensuous sound of his voice reminded Mandy of whose heart was destined not to heal. "Last night he told us—or rather, Iris told us—his place was ransacked, just like Mandy's."

"Your place was ransacked, too?" Bill asked.

"Earlier. While you were busy arresting Jack."

"Oh, Lordy, I've botched this one but good. Try to treat some out-of-towners nicely, and look what happens."

"I'm an out-of-towner," Jack complained. "You didn't treat me nicely."

"And now I'm apologizing. Tell me what needs to be done, folks. I can file charges against these con men, only I've got to tell you, the names they gave me were false."

"Surprise, surprise," Mandy drawled.

"I'll put them in the computer anyway. I wish I could run 'em in, but they're long gone."

"Where did they go?" Jack asked.

"I reckon back where they came from—New York."

Jack turned to Mandy, looking absurdly thrilled. "That's it, then. They've gone to New York. I'll go after them."

"Why in tarnation do you want to go after them?" Bill asked.

"Because they have—something of mine," Jack said discreetly. "It's nothing to do with you, Mc-Intyre. It's between me and them." His gaze remained on Mandy. "Are you sure you don't want to come along for the ride?"

She met his gaze. She wondered if he could see her anguish in her eyes, her yearning to hear him tell her he loved her and needed her with him.

If he saw it, he refused to satisfy it. "It's up to you" was all he said.

She lowered her eyes. Jack had already taken her for a ride. She had enough sense to get off when she had the chance. "No, Jack. I'm staying here."

He said nothing for a minute, then turned to stare past her at her truck. "Okay."

Okay. Just like that. He could take her or leave her. *Okay.*

"I reckon you're going to want me to drive you back to Huntington," she mumbled, even though the prospect of spending any extra time with him made her want to weep.

He seemed to sense her dismay. "If you could drop me off in town, I could call a cab."

"A cab!" Bill hooted. "Where do you-all think you are? Listen, son, you need a ride anywhere, I'll take you there. It's the least I owe you."

"I don't know, I—"

"Let him take you," Mandy recommended.

Again Jack paused before speaking. Again, in a low, inscrutable voice, he said, "Okay." She felt his eyes on her, his hand nearing her, and then he abruptly turned and stalked to the truck parked outside the barn. "Let's hit the road, Bill. I've got some business to clear up before I can go home."

Go home, Mandy thought, watching bitterly as the two men climbed into the Bronco. Jack stared out the passenger window at her, his eyes appearing less bright than they'd been when she had awakened beside him. Much less bright than they'd been in the darkest shadows of the night, when he'd locked his body to hers and unlocked all the love inside her.

Maybe he was disappointed that she wasn't willing to tag along to New York with him like a loyal pet, anxious to help him track down his cursed doll. Maybe he'd expected that she needed nothing more than the most superficial invitation to put her life on hold and scamper off for a few days of fun and games with him.

Well, he was wrong. Last night, she would have gone anywhere with him. Last night, she was sure he loved her the way she loved him.

This morning she knew better.

Chapter Eight

Something's gone wrong here, he thought.

He continued to stare out the wide square window of Bill McIntyre's Bronco long after they'd bounced their way back to the paved road and Mandy was no longer in view. She was still in Jack's own private view, inside him, an afterimage permanently burned into his mind.

Why hadn't she leapt at the chance to come to New York with him?

And why should he care that she hadn't? It wasn't as if he was in love with her or anything. He liked her, he admired her, he considered her sensational in bed— or, more accurately, on a heap of cushions in a barn loft—but he had no interest in anything big and heavy and long-term with her.

If this morning had to be their farewell, though, he wished it could have been a little friendlier. Maybe a hug, a kiss on the cheek...another go-round under that cozy quilt, on those thick, soft, cushions....

Making love with her had remedied all the bruises he'd suffered during his trying day, all the stiffness and soreness, all the exhaustion and rage. It had put him back together. When at last he and Mandy had quieted down for the night, he'd slept like the proverbial baby, a deep, healing sleep. He'd awakened feeling surprisingly well rested, alert and clearheaded, prepared to face the next challenge to his claim on the Moe doll.

It would have been nice if she'd agreed to face that challenge with him.

Of course, her brother's convalescence was a legitimate concern—although that punk-styled, platinum-haired ex-wife of Jessie's seemed to have matters well in hand. Iris had vowed to make the guy soup. What more could Mandy do for him?

That train of thought led Jack back to the depot he'd prefer to avoid: that she'd only been using Jessie's injuries as an excuse to stay in Kentucky. That she would have used any excuse at all not to go to spend any more time with Jack.

That she'd only been using Jack.

"I tell you," Bill remarked with a shake of the head, "Harrow just ain't used to this sort of activity. We haven't had so many New Yorkers in town at one time since a Civilian Conservation Corps bus broke down en route to Tennessee in 1934."

"Will she be all right?" he blurted out.

"Who? Mandy?"

"Yeah. Those bastards told you they were returning to New York, but how do you know they really are? How do you know they're not going to come back and bother her some more?"

"Why do you think they'd do that?"

"They did it once, didn't they?" Jack said carefully. Bill still didn't seem to know what had brought the thugs to town, other than that it hadn't been a Civilian Conservation Corps bus. Jack wasn't going to be the one to spill the beans about what Mandy had tucked snugly inside her bulging purse.

"Well, I reckon they've had their fun terrorizing us folks. But I can't see the purpose in it, and I can't figure they'd have any reason to do it again. There's plenty of other hollers they can go and harass."

"Promise me you'll keep an eye on her," Jack demanded. If he caught up with the thugs in New York, he'd find a way to guarantee that they'd never again come within a hundred miles of her.

If he found them.

If he didn't, though...

Jack's stomach knotted up. If anything happened to her, anything at all... "Promise me, Bill. Promise me you'll protect her with your life. I don't think she's out of danger yet."

"Mandy knows how to take care of herself," Bill declared, his porcine face marked by a frown.

"Those guys had a gun—"

"You ever see Mandy use that shotgun o' hers? Last year she took a ribbon in target shooting at the county fair."

"She did?" Jack would be the first to admit she'd looked damned competent, not to say irresistibly sexy, waving her shotgun around. But he was reassured to hear she could actually use it.

"She knows how to protect herself," Bill muttered, sounding keenly disappointed. "Nobody gets too close to her. And it ain't for lack of trying."

"What do you mean?"

"I mean, there ain't a man in the county who hasn't tried his luck with her. Ever since she came home from Georgia a few years back, every single man—and a few not-so-single ones—have tried their damnedest to catch her fancy. She won't have none of it."

"I take it you're among those who tried their damnedest," Jack guessed.

Bill's cheeks darkened from pink to red. "Can you blame me? She's one hell of a foxy-lookin' lady. But no, she ain't interested in me or anyone else. If it weren't for the fact that she had herself a man in Atlanta, folks around here might think she was . . . you know, abnormal or something. But it ain't that. It's just, she's untouchable."

She hadn't been untouchable last night. She'd let Jack touch her anywhere and everywhere, and she'd joyously touched him right back.

Had he truly been her first man in years? The possibility astounded him—and helped to explain her standoffishness this morning. She wasn't the sort of woman who slept around, who indulged in lighthearted affairs. When at long last she did make love to a man, it meant something.

Damn. He should have told her it meant something to him, too. He should have assured her that, whatever it was they'd found in each other's arms last night, it hadn't been a lighthearted affair. She mattered to him. Last night he'd needed her the way he'd never needed a woman before.

Maybe he still needed her this morning.

He would call her as soon as he got back to New York. That was it: he'd call and tell her how very much last night had meant to him.

Except that she had an unlisted telephone number, and she hadn't bothered to tell him what it was.

"Bill," he began, turning in his seat, "you know her phone number, don't you?"

"Mandy's? I know it as an officer of the law in Harrow, Kentucky, but it ain't my prerogative to pass it around."

"I know, but . . . it would really mean a lot to me if you could see your way to sharing it." He ostentatiously pulled his wallet out of his pocket. Mandy had told him Bill McIntyre could be bought.

Bill eyed the wallet the way a diabetic might eye a chocolate bar. "Don't even think about it, Slater. You offer me money, I gotta arrest you. And I think it would be better all around if you just went back to where you came from, don't you?"

One night of wild drinking, one remorseful morning after, and Bill had apparently found his way back to the straight and narrow. Jack folded his wallet and stuffed it into the hip pocket of his jeans. He didn't want to spend another minute in that ghastly holding cell.

"What do you want her phone number for, anyway?" Bill pressed him. "Don't tell me you're volunteering to be the next man she rejects."

She didn't reject me, Jack almost objected, although that morning she *had* rejected him. "Mandy and I have unfinished business," he said, which wasn't a complete lie.

"Mandy Harlon decides for herself what business is worth finishing," Bill declared with finality. "If she wants to finish your business, she'll let you know. If not, forget it."

"I hardly think you ought to be giving me advice about how to deal with her."

"I've known her a helluva lot longer than you have, son. She don't do any business she don't want to do. Her mother was a Southern belle, her father's parents were backwoods oddballs—her grandfather being a moonshiner, and her grandmother a doll maker, just like her—and pardon me for speaking my mind, but she inherited the worst of both families. She wound up beautiful and stuck-up. She thinks she's better'n everyone."

"She *is* better than everyone," Jack argued, wondering why he was so eager to defend her. It wasn't as if Bill McIntyre posed a threat to her. For that matter, it wasn't as if Bill had said anything demonstrably false about her. She hadn't seemed stuck-up to Jack, but she was beautiful and headstrong.

And if Jack had a scrap of self-preservation in him, he'd put her out of his mind.

He'd asked her to come to New York with him. She'd said no, loud and clear. Even after a couple of punches to the head in that ruckus last night, his brain was functioning well enough to remind him that, as far as Mandy was concerned, their business was definitely finished.

SHE'D PUT IT OFF *long enough.*

First Mandy had stopped to straighten up Jessie's cabin and repair the damage done by the thugs. Now she had no choice but to go home.

But going home meant confronting her life—a life without Jack Slater in it. It meant accepting that her little adventure with him had come to an end.

As she pulled the truck into her driveway and noted the ruts in her front yard from when she'd driven the truck around the thugs' car, memories of the previous day crowded her. She recalled Jack hunkering down in the driveway, piercing the thugs' tires with his pocketknife. She recalled him vaulting into the back of the truck while bullets whizzed past his head.

He could have died.

He could have died earlier, too, when he drove off the cliff. And later, when he fought with the gunman in the hospital parking lot.

She ordered herself not to think about it. Jack was very much alive and on his way home. If she cared all that much about him, she could have extended their time together by a couple of days and flown up to New York with him. It could have been fun.

Damn it. She didn't want fun with Jack.

What she wanted he wasn't offering.

With a desolate sigh, she got out of the truck and swung open her perpetually unlocked front door. She'd been back to the house before she'd gotten Jack out of jail the previous afternoon, so she knew what to expect. Even so, at the sight of the mayhem, she wondered if she was going to cry. She remained stoically dry-eyed, however. This was only a mess. Tears were for *real* tragedies.

Like losing Jack.

She felt her eyes burn with moisture at that thought. Dear God, why had she sent him away? Had she really needed to hear him say he loved her before she could run off with him?

Yes. And he hadn't said it. Maybe he couldn't.

On the other hand, maybe he'd said it in his own way: by forfeiting his doll and saving her life outside the hospital last night. By leaving without even mentioning the possibility that he had earned a share of the diamonds she still had in her possession.

After all he'd been through, he'd wound up empty-handed. No doll, no diamonds, no honey-pie to accompany him to New York.

All right, she thought, righting one of the heavy bolts and wrapping the unraveled cloth around it. Even if Jack didn't love her, she owed him her life. At the very least, she owed him his doll.

She concentrated her energies on her workbench first, checking the sewing machine for damage, scooping up the spools and snipping off the frayed and tangled threads. All the while, her brain churned.

She was going to get Jack his doll. He had paid her for it. She was obligated to make sure he got it. Even if it meant she had to travel to New York City, after all.

In fact, there was no way Jack could get his doll without her. He didn't know who the thugs were, and he didn't have the name and address of Albert Stevenson, her quartz-crystal supplier, the man who had hired the thugs to go after her.

She had his name and address. She would get the doll from Albert Stevenson and give it to Jack.

And then she would say goodbye and return to Harrow. She wasn't going to force her way into his life, or try to make him feel for her what she felt for him. She was only going to give him what he'd come to her for. Fair was fair, and customer satisfaction was paramount.

It was well past four o'clock by the time she tied up the last sack of garbage from the house. The next sack she dealt with was the one that held the diamonds.

She loosened the drawstring and shook out a handful of stones. But the thought of sifting the diamonds from the quartz made her weary. With a sigh, she tossed the loose stones back into the bag and knotted the string.

What was she going to do with them?

She couldn't take the diamonds with her to New York City. She had never been to New York before, but she surmised that strolling down Broadway with several million dollars in jewels stowed in one's purse wasn't a wise idea.

Bill McIntyre might have experienced a change of heart, but Mandy didn't trust him. She trusted Jessie, but the diamonds had already brought him enough grief.

She dialed Bobby Lee's private office number.

"Bobby Lee, it's me. Mandy."

"Mandy!" he said brightly. "Well, darlin', to what do I owe the honor?"

She wasted no time. "I need your help, Bobby. I've come into some diamonds."

"Diamonds? Real diamonds?"

"I believe so."

"How many is 'some'?"

"There's a lot, Bobby Lee. They're mixed in with a mess of rose-quartz crystals." She related to him the events of the past two days—without a mention of

Jack Slater. She wasn't prepared to answer any questions on that particular subject.

Other than to needle her some about her New Age dolls—"Those crazy witch friends of yours really got you hooked on that nonsense, didn't they?"—Bobby Lee listened patiently to her explanation. "It seems obvious these stones are tainted in some way," he said. "Most likely, they've been smuggled into the country to avoid import taxes."

"That's what we thought."

"We? Who's we?"

Mandy winced. "Me and Jessie," she improvised.

"I see. You went to your savvy and sophisticated big brother for advice before you came to me."

"I went to him because he's kin," she said pointedly.

Bobby Lee had the decency to back down. "Here's what I recommend. Perhaps you're familiar with that grand old expression, 'possession is nine-tenths of the law.'"

"I've heard it."

"Then we can fairly say your claim to these diamonds is ninety percent assured."

"Fine. But things get complicated, Bobby Lee—"

"Things are already complicated," he interrupted.

"They get worse. I've got to leave town for a few days."

"Why? Where are y'all headed?"

"To New York. I can't take the diamonds with me, and I don't know what to do with them, short of burying them in the backyard. And with the spring thaw, I reckon that's a lousy idea."

"It would be a lousy idea without the spring thaw," Bobby Lee confirmed. "Why don't you put them in a safe-deposit box at your bank?"

Mandy snorted. "The local bank in Harrow is gossip central. If I walked in there and asked for a safe-deposit box, that would be the subject of discussion for the next few months, at least."

"All right, all right. Here's what you do. Send the diamonds to me, and I'll put them in a bank here. It's probably safer that way, too, everything nice and relatively anonymous. Would you like me to do that for you?"

Mandy might have seen her romance with Bobby Lee go up in smoke, but she had always trusted him. And she told him so.

"All right. Now y'all pack them up and send them to me, overnight mail. Don't insure the package, or you'll have to tell the post office what's inside, and that won't do. Make photocopies and send me the originals of any documentation you might have to prove that the shipment belongs to you. I'll lock the whole shebang up in a safe-deposit box and express-mail you the key."

"Are you sure you don't mind doing this for me?" Mandy asked.

Bobby Lee laughed. "If these diamonds are real, I might just bill you for my services. Two-fifty an hour, darlin'. Given what the diamonds must be worth, I'm sure y'all can afford it.''

"Two dollars and fifty cents?" She deliberately misunderstood him. "I might be able to scare up that kind of money."

"Why are you going to New York, if I may ask?"

She considered her answer, then opted for the truth. If she was going to trust Bobby Lee with her diamonds, she ought to trust him with the whole story. "I'm going after the supplier, Bobby Lee. His henchmen stole a custom-made doll from me, and I've got to get it back."

"Mandy—"

She heard the reproach in his tone. "I've got to," she insisted. "I've got to return it to the man who owns it."

"That sounds dangerous."

"I'm not scared." To her amazement, she wasn't.

"Then you're a fool."

"Can't argue with that."

"Why can't you just make the man another doll?"

Because I love him. "Because the doll is for his foster father who's got arthritis and thinks the quartz is going to cure him."

Bobby Lee issued a pungent curse. "I'll look up your witch friends and have them cast a spell to protect you. Do me a favor, Mandy—be careful."

She smiled. "It's nice to know you still care."

"Hell, I don't care," he teased. "All I'm worried about is, if something happens to you, I'll have a heck of a tough time getting access to the safe-deposit box."

"Oh, for heaven's sake, Bobby Lee! I'm not going to get killed."

"Famous last words."

"I hope not."

"So do I," he said quietly, no trace of mockery in his tone. "Be careful, love-bunch. I don't want to read about you in the tabloids."

"If I *do* wind up there, your parents won't be surprised. They always thought I'd end up in a scandal."

She bade him goodbye, leaned back in her chair, and propped her feet up on the workbench, the diamonds resting in her lap. And worked out her strategy.

She wasn't going to pressure Jack. She wasn't going to throw herself at him. She wasn't going to tell him that she was in love with him.

She was simply going to get the doll, give it to him, and vanish.

If she didn't, she'd never be able to get on with her life. She'd never get over Jack. Like Jessie's jaw, her heart would be wired shut, caged, immobile, locked away forever.

She had to get the doll. Not just for Jack, but for herself.

Chapter Nine

Mandy wondered how Jack could possibly think the mountain roads of Kentucky were crazy. Compared to New York City, motoring around Harrow seemed like a downright sedate activity.

She had spent nearly an hour in the back seat of a yellow cab, watching her life flash before her eyes, as it was supposed to when one was having a near-death experience.

Mandy clutched the strap of her duffel bag and prayed.

When the driver finally came to a stop at the curb, she peered out the window. Something was wrong.

"Excuse me," she called to the driver through the Plexiglas divider. "Are you sure this is the address I gave you?"

"*Sí, sí*. This address."

She gazed out the window again. The shops lining the sidewalks had signs printed in Chinese. A bank at the corner resembled a pagoda. Even the telephone booth had several ornate triangular roofs rising from it.

She pulled out the slip of paper with her supplier's address on it and read it once more. "This is Mott Street?" she shouted through the divider.

"*Sí,* is Mott Street."

With a sigh, she handed the driver two twenty dollar bills and got out of the cab.

So this was Chinatown. The window she stood in front of was filled with all manner of exotic vegetables and herbs, above which hung a neat row of scrawny, smoked fowl, plucked and shiny with grease. Not at all unlike the chickens Gramma Harlon used to behead and pluck in the backyard.

Searching for the address, she strolled past a shop displaying gorgeous embroidered silk and delicate ivory carvings and what appeared to be an opium den, although she knew those no longer existed. Inside the door a group of elderly men played mah-jongg in the dim light while incense burned all around them.

Why Albert Stevenson would run his business in Chinatown was beyond her.

On the next block she found the address she was looking for, a drab tenement occupying several stories above a shoe-repair shop. Up narrow, dimly lit stairs to the third floor she found apartment 3-B and knocked.

A minute passed, and then the door opened as far as a safety chain would allow. A short, elderly woman peeked out. "Yes?"

Mandy squinted in the dusky light. The woman appeared harmless. No more than five feet tall, she had a face as creased as a peach pit, and thin gray hair.

Mandy offered her warmest Southern smile. "Hi. I'm looking for Mr. Stevenson. Might he be in?"

"He might be, but he isn't."

"I'm here on business," Mandy added, shifting her duffel bag on her shoulder so it was less visible.

"Nobody around here engages in any business with women as young as you."

"No, *real* business," Mandy insisted. "He has a doll of mine, and—"

The woman slammed the door shut.

Mandy took a deep breath and knocked again.

The elderly woman cracked it open. "Please," Mandy said. "I don't want to cause any trouble. All I want is the doll, and then I'll disappear."

"What doll?"

The woman had to know exactly what doll they were talking about. If she didn't, she wouldn't have slammed the door a minute ago.

Mandy weighed her response carefully and opted to play for sympathy. "It's a handmade doll, and it belongs to a client of mine. He paid for it, and if I don't get it to him, I'll have to make another one, and I just don't know if I can make one as good. Please, ma'am, just give me the doll and I'll be on my way."

"Listen to me," the woman said, her tone growing intense as she pressed her nose into the space between the door and the wall. "You look like a nice kid. Do yourself a favor and get the hell out of here."

A frisson of fear raced down Mandy's spine, but she ignored it. "I'll leave once I have my doll back."

"You don't get it," the woman whispered. "Forget the doll. It's gone. And if you're not gone by the time he gets back, he's gonna get the rest of the stuff from you. Now beat it." She closed the door with a decisive click.

Mandy took another deep breath and coughed out the dust. The woman's words sank in: Albert Stevenson was on his way here. If the elderly woman knew who Mandy was, Stevenson would surely know. He'd do to her what his henchmen had failed to do down in Kentucky. And since Mandy didn't have the diamonds on her, he'd do whatever was necessary to find out where they were. Like torture her. Or hold her for ransom.

Jack had been smart to say they should hire a bodyguard. *They.* She should have done this with Jack. She should have come to New York with him, even if he didn't love her, even if he made no promises for a future beyond the moment he had his doll back. She should have had him by her side when it was time to face her supplier.

At least that way, if her death was imminent, she would have been able to tell him she loved him.

She heard footsteps on the stairway two stories below, and imminent death no longer seemed like a morbid fantasy. Swallowing her fear, she peeked over the railing. She saw a steel gray mane of hair—the top of a man's head.

He looked big.

She darted to a window at the end of the hall, and climbed out onto a fire escape. Pressing herself against the sooty brownstone wall, she edged close enough to the window to spy in.

The big man entered apartment 3-B and closed the door behind him.

Hoisting her duffel bag higher on her back, Mandy scampered down the metal fire-escape ladders to the alley at the rear of the building. Picking a path through the assorted trash that covered the ground, she worked her way out to a side street and then back to Mott Street, to the alien, aroma-laden world of Chinatown.

She kept walking, fearful that the man or the woman might come after her. She kept her gaze straight ahead, refusing to let the exotic sights and sounds distract her.

At last she reached a huge, bustling boulevard. To her left loomed a huge suspension bridge swarming with road traffic. A sign on the corner read Canal Street.

She paused to catch her breath.

Around her teemed hundreds of people. Trucks spewed exhaust fumes, a jackhammer chattered against the pavement. Closing her eyes, she pictured Jack. She imagined his dark hair, his darker eyes, his lean body, his husky laugh and arrogant attitude. She thought of the first time she'd seen him, when he'd sauntered into her house and demanded his doll, and of his second invasion of her house, wet and bedraggled and bleeding. She thought of his determination, his courage, his tough exterior belying his concern for his foster father and Jessie—and her.

She thought of the way his body had felt next to hers, inside her, loving her.

And the way she'd felt the next morning, when he'd been hatching his new scheme for getting his doll back, instead of telling her what she desperately wanted to hear.

Now she was on his turf, and she didn't know what to do.

From the pocket of her denim jacket she pulled out a paper: the photocopy of the order form for the doll from Dido. The order form had both Jack's and Moe Kaplan's names on it, but only one address. She didn't know whether it was Jack's or Moe's.

Not that it mattered. She had nowhere else to go—other than back to the airport.

Amid the rushing traffic on Canal Street she spotted a few yellow cabs. If she'd been brave enough to knock on Stevenson's door, she supposed she could be brave enough to tempt fate with another cab ride.

Once again when she arrived at the address, she felt as if she were in a foreign land. Not Chinatown this time, but Upper Crustville. A woman in a black silk slacks suit, silver shoes and an ocean's worth of pearls strolled down the street, walking a toy poodle decked

out in a rhinestone-studded collar. When Mandy took
a deep breath this time, her lungs filled with the
woman's pricey perfume.

She went up a short flight of stairs to the carved oak
front door of the town house. Whoever lived here
must be incredibly rich. Richer than she would have
guessed Jack to be.

A middle-aged woman in a housedress answered the
door. "Yes?"

"Hi," Mandy said, sounding far more confident
than she felt. "My name is Amanda Harlon, and..."
A shadow in motion behind the woman caught Mandy's eye. Someone had entered the hallway. A man.

"Who is it, Nadine?" he called. Not Jack's voice.

As the man came down the hall toward the door, he
grew visible. He was shorter than Jack, with thick silver hair, black eyebrows, a nose as triangular as a
scarecrow's and a tenuous smile.

He looked exactly like his doll. "Moe Kaplan!" she
blurted out. "I'm Amanda Harlon."

"Mandy Harlon!" He swept past the woman who'd
answered the door and gathered Mandy's right hand
in both of his. His hands were as gnarled as Jack had
described them, his joints swollen with the arthritis
that the doll was supposed to cure. "Come in, come
in! Who would have thought? Come in, sweetheart.
Make us some tea, Nadine."

Mandy was led into the marble-floored hallway,
past an ornate staircase and into a parlor decorated
with understated elegance. Leather-bound books lined

the walls; the carved mantle above the fireplace was cluttered with Depression glass bottles; the floor was covered in a thick, faded Persian rug and the furniture looked plush and heavy and obscenely comfortable.

She set down her duffel bag and sank into one of the armchairs. It was even more comfortable than it looked. Then again, at this point she would have found sitting on a pile of twigs comfortable.

Moe took a seat on a plump sofa across a sturdy mahogany coffee table from her. He laced his twisted fingers together and smiled beatifically at her.

"You-all know who I am," she concluded.

"I most certainly do." His New York accent was much more pronounced than Jack's. His smile was grandfatherly.

"Did Jack tell you about me?"

"He told me some. And listen, sweetheart, I've got to tell you, those dolls of yours really work. I have a friend, his sister bought one of your dolls for her daughter, at Dido, and next thing you know, the daughter is accepted into Cornell University."

"My dolls can't get anyone into college," Mandy protested with a laugh.

"A word to the wise, dear. Don't build your advertising campaign around that."

Nadine arrived, carrying a tray of tea things. She poured two cups, then left the room.

Mandy eyed the tea, and then the plate of cookies next to it. She was famished. The flight attendant had served a snack somewhere above Virginia, but Mandy had been too anxious to eat.

Moe seemed delighted when she helped herself to a couple of cookies. "So, you came to New York, after all," he said.

"After all what?"

"Jack said he'd invited you to come with him and you turned him down."

She detected a tiny hint of disapproval in his tone. "I didn't exactly turn him down. My brother was ailing." *And Jack and I had just spent a night making love,* she added silently, *and all he could think of the next morning was his doll.*

"So, how's your brother? Why don't you make him a doll?"

"He doesn't need a doll. He's got Iris." Mandy licked a crumb off her thumb, then took a sip of hot tea. "I really want to get your doll for you, Mr. Kaplan. That's why I'm here. Not because Jack asked me to come." *In spite of his asking me to come,* she muttered under her breath.

Moe stirred a cube of sugar into his cup, his spoon making a delicate tinkling noise against the exquisite china and his shrewd brown eyes never leaving her. "Jack's a fine boy, you know."

"He thinks very highly of you, too," she said.

Moe sipped his tea, then lowered his cup. "This isn't a mutual-admiration society, Miss Harlon. I'm talking life and death here. Jack is an amazing human being."

Mandy felt her cheeks grow warm at her own particular recollections of how amazing Jack could be. But she didn't want to hear Moe Kaplan sing Jack's praises. She didn't want to be in love with him. She only wanted to resolve her business and go home.

"Not that he needs me tooting his horn for him, but this is a horn that ought to be tooted. I don't know why you turned Jack down, but I'm glad you changed your mind."

"I didn't change my mind."

"But you're here."

"For the doll. Not for Jack."

"You should be here for Jack," Moe chided. "He hasn't been happy since he got back from Tennessee."

"Tennessee?"

"Or is it Kentucky? I get them confused."

"I'm sorry he hasn't been happy," she said dryly, "but I'm sure once we get your doll back—" *and he gets his hands on all the diamonds inside it* "—his spirits will improve."

"The hell with the doll," Moe snorted with a dismissive wave of his hand. "I'm fighting for that boy, Miss Harlon. His happiness is my prime concern. I owe him my life, you know."

"Oh?" The way Jack had described it, Moe had been the one to save Jack's life.

"I was a lonely man before Jack showed up at my front door. My dear wife Lily, God rest her soul, had never been able to have children. When she passed away, I had nothing left but my work. I made a lot of money, Miss Harlon, but I was a sad, sad man until one cold night when a skinny ragamuffin with a huge chip on his shoulder turned up on my porch. That boy needed me in a way no one had needed me since Lily died. And there is nothing more important in this world than being needed.''

Mandy hadn't expected to spend teatime discussing the meaning of life with Moe Kaplan. Then again, she hadn't expected any of the things that had happened to her since Jack had turned up at *her* front door.

But everything had happened.

''And now,'' Moe said quietly, ''I think Jack needs you.''

She smiled wistfully and shook her head. ''I don't mean to be contrary, Mr. Kaplan, but you're wrong. If he needed me...'' *He would have told me. He would have begged me to stay by his side.* ''What-all did he tell you about his trip to Kentucky?''

''Not much,'' Moe admitted with a wily grin. ''Just enough.'' He drained his cup and set it down in its saucer. ''I'm having a dinner party tonight, Miss Harlon. Jack and some other friends. Why don't you come, too?''

''And see Jack? Tonight?'' She hadn't planned to cross paths with him until she had the doll back. And then only to hand it over and say goodbye.

''You could spend the night here if you'd like. Unless, of course, you've made other arrangements.''

Mandy was ashamed to admit she hadn't. "I was planning to stay in a motel for the night."

"A motel? In Manhattan?" He threw back his head and guffawed. "There's no such animal, sweetheart. Hotels only, most of them charging on the order of two hundred dollars a night. Now, can I interest you in a room upstairs? Private bath and breakfast included."

Mandy thought of her stash of diamonds in a safe-deposit box in Atlanta. If the diamonds remained in her possession, she'd be rich enough to afford any room in any hotel in the city, for as long as she wanted. But the diamonds might have to be turned over to the authorities.

"Thank you," she said. "I'd like to stay here, if I might."

Her accent seemed to amuse Moe. "You might," he assured her, rising to his feet. "Nadine?"

The housekeeper appeared in the arched doorway.

"Could you please take Miss Harlon to one of the guest bedrooms upstairs? She'll be spending the night here. Oh, and we'll be a couple more for dinner tonight."

"Okay," Nadine said, gesturing for Mandy to follow her.

As she trailed Nadine up the stairs, Mandy puzzled over Moe's final instructions to the housekeeper. A *couple* more for dinner? Mandy wasn't planning to eat enough for two.

But she was too tired to care what he'd meant.

"TONIGHT?" Jack stared at his calendar, which had nothing but the date written on it. He focused on the blank white page and wondered when he was going to be able to think clearly again. Ever since he'd left Kentucky, his mind had been as empty as that day on his calendar.

Except for thoughts of Mandy.

"Yes, tonight." Moe's voice resounded through the telephone wire. "I'm having the Lazars over, and Kitty and Lewis Martin, Mike McCormick, Betsy Rudolph... Just a few people, nothing fancy. Nadine's making a roast."

"I don't know."

"What, you've got other plans? You've got a date?"

Jack scowled. Moe knew damned well Jack didn't have a date. Jack had only had to make the mistake of mentioning Mandy Harlon's name once or twice, and Moe had immediately jumped to conclusions.

Unfortunately, they were the right conclusions.

"So, what are you going to do tonight? Sit around and mope in your apartment? Come over. Be sociable. You know Betsy Rudolph has a crush on you."

Betsy Rudolph had been Moe's wife's best friend. In her sixties, she sat on a dozen boards, ran three charities, went out with men in their forties and flirted with men in their thirties, like Jack. She was basically harmless, and usually amusing.

So were the other guests Moe had mentioned. Nadine was a good cook. And Moe was right: if Jack didn't go to Moe's house for dinner, he'd probably spend the night sitting around moping. "All right," he relented. "I'll be there."

"Good. Seven o'clock. Nothing fancy," Moe instructed him, then hung up before Jack could change his mind.

He sighed and lowered the receiver. Swiveling his chair, he gazed unseeing at the broad corner windows, at the balmy late-afternoon sunshine April carried into his office.

The whole time he'd been with Mandy, it had rained. And suddenly sunshine didn't seem so appetizing.

Since returning to New York three days ago, he'd tried without success to scare up her phone number. He'd badgered the manager at Dido and the Lawrence County directory assistance, but neither would release her number. He'd gotten Jessie's number from the directory assistance, but no one answered at his house. Jack wondered whether Jessie had moved in with Iris or simply couldn't talk.

He'd considered hiring a private investigator, but that seemed sleazy. Instead he sent her a note. Letter writing wasn't his forte, so all he'd written were his own phone numbers at work and home and a plea for her to call him. "We've got to talk," he'd scrawled, along with his name.

He'd mailed the letter yesterday, which meant she would probably get it tomorrow. Which, in turn, meant that, starting tomorrow, he would be spending the bulk of his time staring at his telephone and wishing it would ring.

How had he gotten himself into this funk?

His secretary swept in with a stack of contracts for him to review, and he forced himself to deal with professional matters for the rest of the day. Still catching up from the workdays he'd missed during his brief jaunt to Kentucky, he wound up staying late at the office. His subway line was suffering one of its typical unexplained delays, and after standing at the platform for twenty minutes he decided to skip going home and head directly to Moe's house across town. So what if he looked rumpled? So what if he wasn't freshly shaved? Moe was entertaining his own friends, not Jack's, and none of them were people he had to impress.

He crossed the platform to catch the crosstown shuttle train, then caught the number-five train uptown. It was a few minutes past seven when he rang Moe's bell.

Nadine opened the door and accepted a friendly kiss on the cheek from the man she'd helped Moe to usher through a troubled adolescence into healthy adulthood. "Everyone's upstairs in the living room," she told him. "Go on up. I've got stuff to see to in the kitchen."

Nodding, Jack tugged the knot of his tie a bit looser and unbuttoned his collar. He loped up the stairs two at a time, thinking about the beer Moe always kept stocked in the wet-bar refrigerator in his study down the hall from the living room. He heard amiable chatter drifting out into the hall, Betsy Rudolph's boisterous laughter, Lewis Martin pontificating on some subject about which he undoubtedly knew less than he thought he knew. With a sigh, Jack bypassed the study to say hello to the guests.

But he saw only one guest. Dressed in a simple sheath of turquoise that ended above her knees and had buttons down the front, she stood to the side, looking shy, out of place—and utterly radiant. Her hair flared around her face like wildfire, and her eyes reflected the blue of her dress, and her legs were astonishingly shapely in stockings and modest high heels . . . and his attention returned to those buttons down the front of her dress.

He imagined plucking them open, one by one.

He lifted his gaze to her face just as she glanced at the door. When their eyes met, she started and caught her lower lip in her teeth.

He didn't know how she'd gotten to Moe's house. He didn't know why. And he didn't care.

All that mattered was that she was here.

Chapter Ten

She had spent the past twenty minutes listening to a statuesque older woman named Betsy discuss a non-profit crafts organization on whose board she sat. Her haute couture dress displaying a figure any teenager would be proud of, her neck lassoed in ropes of gold and her earlobes winking with rubies, Betsy went on and on about how the organization was overrun with ceramists and utterly lacking in doll makers. "I understand doll making is a craft as old as this nation," she said.

"Older," Mandy informed her.

"And passed from generation to generation. That's what truly distinguishes it. Are you the daughter of a doll maker?"

"The granddaughter," Mandy said, clutching her wineglass so it wouldn't slip and crash onto the glossy parquet floor. She wasn't much of a wine drinker, and on those rare occasions when she did drink wine, it was usually out of a jelly jar, not an etched-crystal goblet. "In my family, doll making skipped a generation."

"I wonder if I could interest you in presenting a lecture at our next conference. If I have to listen to one more speech on advances in pottery-wheel design, I shall scream."

At that moment Mandy saw Jack standing in the doorway—and she very nearly screamed herself.

She had known he would be here. For what had remained of the afternoon, as she'd dozed on the bed Moe had so generously offered her, as she'd showered and shampooed her hair and then unpacked the one dress she'd had the foresight to toss into her bag before she'd left Harrow, she'd thought about little else but seeing Jack.

When, at seven o'clock, Nadine had tapped on her door and asked if she would like to come downstairs to join the other guests for a cocktail, she had known that he might very well be standing at the bottom of the staircase, waiting for her. That he hadn't been only fueled her anxiety. She would rather have gotten the reunion over with.

Instead she'd had to mingle with Moe's guests, making small talk and pretending she wasn't preoccupied with thoughts of Jack, his impending arrival, what she was going to do when she saw him.

Now she knew what she was going to do: devour him with her gaze. Memorize every detail of him, from his tousled brown hair to his deep-set eyes, to his thin lips and sharp jaw, his loosened tie and wrinkled shirt, his tailored trousers and moccasin-stitched loafers. Then her gaze was going to travel back up again, to his face, his mouth, his chin—did the man never shave? she wondered, observing the five-o'clock shadow contouring his cheeks, exactly as it had the morning at the barn when they'd parted ways—and his eyes. His dark, burning eyes.

She couldn't tell whether he was glad to see her. "Glad" definitely didn't describe her own emotional state. Her nerves twitched and twittered beneath her skin, and her stomach lurched, and her breath got stuck in her throat. Her hands became so cold she had to put down her glass and rub her fingertips together to restore the circulation in them.

Betsy, on the other hand, seemed delighted by his arrival. "Jack!" she sang out as she waltzed across the room in her spike-heeled shoes. "Jack, you look more gorgeous every time I see you!"

Jack flashed Betsy a genial smile, then zeroed in on Mandy again. His eyes remained on her as Betsy kissed his cheek and hooked her hand through the bend in his elbow, as he bent his head and murmured something to her. She turned back to look at Mandy; her neatly tweezed eyebrows rose and she grinned.

The easy intimacy between Jack and Betsy vexed Mandy.

She spun away from the door and pretended to be engrossed in Lewis Martin's windy oration on the city's schools. She didn't want to watch as Betsy cuddled up to Jack, as she laid claim to him. Mandy didn't want to acknowledge how jealous she was.

Jack didn't love her. She'd already known that when she'd boarded the plane to LaGuardia that morning. She'd come to New York only to give him his doll and write The End on their relationship—something Jack had apparently done the morning after he'd made love to her.

She sensed him behind her an instant before he lowered his hand to her shoulder. Even so, his touch caused her to flinch.

"What are you doing here?" he whispered.

She opened her mouth to answer and discovered she had no voice.

"Come on," he murmured, his lips so close to her ear she felt his breath on her skin, his raw male allure stirring a response deep inside her. Like a puppet under his control, she nodded, begged Lewis's pardon and let Jack guide her out of the living room.

He steered her into a small study at the end of the hall, closed the door behind them, and gathered her to him. His mouth covered hers, coaxing, seducing, doing all the miraculous things he did every time he kissed her. She felt her lips mimicking his, her tongue welcoming his, her gasp filling his mouth as he slid his hands down to her hips and brought her firmly against him.

Kissing him was like magic, like returning home after a long, tiring journey, like awakening to a sunny summer morning with the azaleas in bloom and the air atremble with the chirping of birds. Kissing Jack was like losing herself, giving herself away even though she knew she would get nothing more than this moment in return.

He slid one hand back up her spine and under the thick tumble of her hair to the nape of her neck. His fingers wound through the curls, tilting her head so his tongue could probe further, reach more of her. His breath escaped him in a low groan.

She had to stop him. She had come to New York to bring things to a tidy conclusion, not to prolong their affair. She couldn't afford to fall any more deeply in love with him than she already was.

Mustering every dram of willpower inside her, she wedged her hands between her chest and Jack's and nudged him away.

He drew back without letting go of her. "Hi," he said, his voice hoarse and his breath ragged.

Hi? Just like that, as if they'd seen each other only hours ago? *Hi?*

"Are you and Betsy Rudolph lovers?" she blurted out, then clapped her hands over her mouth and prayed for a lightning bolt to strike her dead right there in Moe Kaplan's cozy oak-paneled study.

Jack's mouth spread in a smile that she found unfortunately beguiling. "No," he answered.

She could feel a blush overheat her cheeks. "I'm sorry. It's none of my business—"

"It's as much your business as your history with ol' Johnny Reb was my business. When it comes to Betsy, you have nothing to worry about."

"I wasn't worried."

"She likes younger men, but not men young enough to be her son."

"We all have our limits."

"Mmm." Jack brushed her brow with a light kiss. "What are yours?"

"I didn't come here to kiss you," she said, loathing the tremor in her tone.

Still he kept his hands on her, his body perilously close to her. "Why did you come?"

"To get your doll. I owe you that much, Jack."

At last his passion seemed to cool. A frown shadowed his face as he appraised her. "You came to New York to get the doll?"

"I wasn't going to keep it. I was going to give it to you."

"That's beside the point," he argued. "How could you do something so dangerous?"

"I didn't realize it was dangerous until..." She hesitated.

His frown grew darker. "Until what? Don't tell me you went after those bozos on your own."

"Not the thugs," she clarified. "The supplier."

"The supplier!" He tightened his grip on her and gave her a slight shake. "He could have killed you, Mandy!"

"Well, he didn't. I'm here, aren't I?"

He relented with a sigh. "Yeah. You're here, thank God. If something had happened to you, if that creep had so much as touched you..." He swore under his breath. "Promise me you'll never do anything that crazy again."

Mandy had already done something much crazier and infinitely more dangerous: she'd fallen in love with Jack. She couldn't let herself think about that now, though. It might depress her. "You-all haven't gone after the doll, have you?"

"How could I? I've been knocking myself out just trying to reach you. You should be getting a letter from me soon, by the way. I mailed it yesterday. I don't know why you have an unlisted phone number. It hasn't done much to protect you, has it?"

No, it hadn't—not from the thugs and not from Jack. "Well, now I'm here," she said quietly. "If you want my supplier's address, I can give it to you."

"What I want right now has nothing to do with your supplier," Jack said in a low, insinuating voice. He pulled her back to him and planted another kiss on her brow, one on the tip of her nose, one on her lips. "Why don't we go back to my place?"

"I'm not going to sleep with you and then say, 'Nice knowing you,' and go back to Kentucky," she protested, once again hearing the tremor in her voice, once again feeling her cheeks flame with color.

"Then don't go back to Kentucky," he said simply. "Don't say it was nice knowing me. Stick around and hate me."

"Do you mean that?" she asked, brightening.

"I'd rather you stuck around and didn't hate me, but I'll take what I can get."

So would Mandy. He might not be ready to admit that he loved her, but at least he had asked her to stay. She was grasping at straws; she knew his casual invitation would never be enough to satisfy her. But at that moment it would have to do.

To her surprise, Moe Kaplan seemed delighted by the news that she and Jack were leaving his dinner party early. "Are you sure you don't want to stay and eat?" he asked.

"We're sure," Jack answered for both of them. "Thanks, Moe."

"Anytime, anytime." He gave Jack's shoulder an affectionate pat, then summoned Nadine to pack Mandy's things for her.

"I can pack my own bag," Mandy muttered, starting toward the stairs.

Jack held her back. "I don't want to let you go," he murmured. "And if we go upstairs together, we'll never leave."

Before she could argue, Nadine appeared on the stairs, carrying Mandy's duffel bag. Before she could think, she was in the back of a cab, cruising across town. Before she could breathe, Jack was kissing her, the doubts dissolving to dust in her mind.

Jack arched his arm around her shoulders and tucked his free hand under her chin, holding her face still. His stubble of beard made her skin tingle as he grazed her lips. "I missed you," he whispered.

She wondered if "I miss you" would ever become "I love you."

The cab braked in front of a stark, boxy apartment building. "Where are we?" she asked as Jack passed the driver some money.

"My place."

"It looks so different from where Moe lives."

"We're on the West Side," he explained, escorting her into the building, past a doorman and through the lobby to an elevator. Mandy would hate living in a building where you had to ride an elevator just to get to your own front door. If this was Jack's home, they were definitely a dreadful match. Maybe it would be better if she left right now—

No. She tried not to think of forever. Even if he broke her heart tomorrow, at least she would have tonight.

The elevator swept them up twenty floors, and then Jack escorted her down a long, nondescript hallway to his apartment. She had only the briefest opportunity to take in her surroundings—sleek modern furniture, a few thirsty houseplants, a few rugs strewn across the hardwood floor—before he swooped her into his arms and carried her to his bedroom.

She would have tonight, she promised herself. She would give Jack her love tonight, and tomorrow, when it was over, she would deal with the loss as best she could. She was made of sturdy mountain stock, hardy

Harlon genes. If the thugs couldn't crush her spirit, neither could Jack.

At least, she hoped he couldn't.

He dropped her onto the center of his king-size bed, then sprawled out beside her and gazed down at her. "This is like a dream come true," he murmured before taking her mouth with his. His tongue slid deep, then retreated on a sigh. He propped himself up on one elbow and traced the edge of her jaw with his fingertips. "Why didn't you come with me when I left Harrow?"

Her vision slipped in and out of focus as her eyes filled with tears. If they spoke the truth now, she wouldn't be able to delude herself, pretending he loved her as much as she loved him. But she couldn't lie to him—and even if it hurt, she didn't want him to lie to her.

"All you cared about was your doll," she said, her voice low and scratchy.

"My doll?" He threw back his head and laughed. "You're the one who's obsessed with the doll."

"Obsessed? I am not!"

"Then why did you come to New York?"

"Because *you're* obsessed with it, and I knew you wouldn't be able to get it without me. I thought, if I went to my supplier and got the doll for you..."

"What?" he goaded her.

"I'd be able to say goodbye to you," she said, her voice growing softer, less certain.

His smile faded. He traced back up her jaw to her temple and brushed a curly tendril from her cheek. "Is that what you want?" he asked. "To say goodbye?"

"No. That's what *you* want." It agonized her to say it, but she had to speak the truth.

"Oh," he said dryly. "That's what *I* want. That's why I begged you to come with me to New York."

"Begged? All you talked about was the damned doll. You said we'd go back to New York and get it," she said, recalling his words from that ghastly morning. "We'd hire a bodyguard and get the doll for Moe. We'd get the diamonds. You paid for the doll, and it was yours, and getting it back was the only thing that mattered to you."

His eyes grew impossibly darker, veiled behind a frown of incomprehension. "I asked you to come with me and you said no. That's what I remember, Mandy."

"That's right," she retorted. "I didn't want to come if all it was about was getting your stupid doll."

He studied her for a minute, reading her expression, trailing his fingers absently through her hair. "But you would have come if it was about something else."

Don't make me say it, she pleaded inwardly. When his eyes continued to bear down on her, she turned away.

He skimmed his hand back to her chin and steered her face back to him. "What? You want me to say I'm crazy about you?"

"Are you?"

"You want me to say I felt like I'd been kicked in the gut when you turned me down? Help me out, Mandy. Tell me what you want me to say, and I'll say it. Because it's true."

"If it's true," she said, "then you'll have to say it in your own words."

"Here are my words," he whispered, bowing to kiss her again. He rose higher onto her and framed her face with his hands. His lips were tender against hers, sweet and seeking. The passion in his kiss was restrained, as if he feared overpowering her.

Yet his gentleness was in its own way overpowering. She threaded her fingers through his thick, soft hair and held him, matching the cautious, questioning forays of his tongue and luring him deeper. If this was his way of saying he loved her, her heart heard him loud and clear.

He sighed again, then rolled onto his side so he could get at the buttons of her dress. He opened them one at a time, still exercising restraint, refusing to pull back the blue cloth until he had unfastened every button all the way to the hem. The pale camisole and half-slip she had on underneath provoked a smile from him. "I like your underwear."

"That sounds a mite odd."

"Nothing odd about it at all." He tugged the sleeves of the dress down her arms and slid it out from under her. Then he ran his hands over the white silk of her camisole, skimming her breasts and watching her nipples stiffen against the fabric. When at last he slipped his hand under the hem and his warm palm came in contact with her midriff, they both gasped.

"Mandy," he groaned, leaning over and pressing his lips to her collarbone. He eased the narrow straps off her shoulders, holding her arms at her sides as he rose above her once more, kissing a path along the lace edge of the camisole.

She groped at his jacket, yanking on it until he leaned back and pulled it off. Her hands moved to his tie, which he quickly disposed of. His fingers raced hers down the front of his shirt, nimbly attacking the buttons. In an instant the shirt was gone.

An instant more, and her camisole was also gone, swept up over her head. Jack ran his hands down from her shoulders to her breasts, where he lingered only long enough to plant seeds of delicious frustration inside her. He wedged his fingers under the elastic of her slip, eased it down, and groaned when he saw her garter belt.

He sketched his fingertips over her hips, over the narrow band of flesh exposed above each stocking and then down her thighs to her knees, to her calves. The lingerie wasn't tarty; everything matched, a uniformly virtuous white. Yet the way Jack reacted . . .

"Give me some words, Mandy," he implored, skimming his hands back up her legs and then down once more, until he was cradling her feet, massaging her ankles, warming her toes. "I'm speechless."

"My mother always said I should wear nice under-things," Mandy explained earnestly, even as she wriggled one foot free and planted it against the steel-hard muscle of his thigh.

He captured the mischievous foot and kissed her instep. "Convey my thanks to your mother," he said, releasing her legs and concentrating on his trousers. As soon as he'd shed them, Mandy had graphic proof of how very much Jack liked her nice underthings.

He took her feet in his hands again, spreading them apart so he could kneel between her legs. His palms felt hot and tickly through her nylons as he caressed her shins, her calves, her thighs. He inched higher, and she was sure he would release the buttons that held the stockings in place. But he bypassed them, leaving her stockings on and stripping off her panties. Sliding his hands beneath her hips, he bowed and touched his mouth to her.

She moaned, shocked by the hot flood of sensation inside her, the frantic tremors of need surging down to where his lips and tongue moved against her. She had never been loved this way before, and the intensity of her pleasure frightened her.

"No," she mouthed, not to Jack but to herself, to the crazed sprinting of her heartbeat and the jagged tempo of her breath. *No,* to the fearsome pressure building inside her, rising, threatening to engulf her like a wave and drag her down into the drowning depths, deeper than she could survive. She clutched the blankets as her body arched wildly. She was coming apart, shattering, disintegrating into keen pulses of ecstasy. Her hoarse, desperate cry spoke of triumph and defeat.

And then there was more. There was Jack, rising onto her, thrusting, filling her again and again. His mouth—the mouth that had done such astonishing things to her—glided over her lips and cheeks. His body cradled hers, inhabited hers, merged with hers in a seamless dance of passion, of hunger and texture and heat. They moved together, rose together to the peak and then soared beyond it, carried on a transcendent surge of energy, of love.

"Mandy," he groaned a long time later, his respiration still erratic, his heart thudding against her breast as he blanketed her body with his. "You're phenomenal."

"Me, or my underwear?" she asked, surprised at how faint her voice sounded.

Chuckling, he pushed himself up high enough to gaze down at her. "Let's find out. Take off the stockings and see how I respond."

"You haven't even caught your breath," she noted. "You can't possibly respond to anything right now."

"Wanna bet I can't?" His eyes sparkled with challenge.

She mirrored his smile. "You're on," she said, lifting her leg, unfastening the nylon and rolling it slowly down her leg.

She had never before realized how much fun it could be to lose a bet.

ALL YOU CARED ABOUT was your doll. . . .

Jack stood in his compact kitchen, slapping together a couple of sandwiches. Having skipped dinner at Moe's, he was famished.

He had insisted that Mandy remain in bed while he fixed them a snack. The truth was, he needed time to recover. The last go-round, while spectacular, had worn him out.

All you cared about was your doll, she had accused him.

How could she have thought such a thing? Hadn't his feelings been obvious when he'd asked her to come to New York? Really, what the hell did women want? Words?

Apparently.

He shook his head and smiled wistfully. Moe Kaplan had given Jack more than he could ever begin to thank Moe for, but one thing that had been missing in Jack's upbringing was some instruction in how to read a woman's mind. Jack had memories of his mother, but they were remote and tenuous—and they had nothing to do with how to know when a woman wanted to hear a man say certain things.

Moe had been a widower. He'd had lady friends, dates, lovers, but Jack hadn't ever gotten to witness the day-in, day-out of male-female relationships. And as for his father...

He piled the sandwiches on a plate, grabbed a couple of napkins and a bottle of wine, and returned to the bedroom. Mandy lay in a curvacious heap under the blanket, her fiery mop of hair splayed across the pillows and her eyes closed. Jack stepped over her garter belt, which had somehow landed on the floor during a tussle. He shook his head again, horrified to think he'd almost lost her just because he'd failed to tell her in plain English how much he wanted her with him.

But he hadn't lost her. Whether she'd come for the doll or for him was irrelevant. What mattered was that she was here. And he wasn't about to let her go.

Setting the plate down on the night table, he nudged her over so he'd have room to sit on the bed. She yawned, stretched, rolled over and nestled deeper into the pillow.

All right, they'd eat later, he thought, shucking his jeans and sliding in under the blanket next to her. He could use a few minutes of sleep himself.

Before he could get her comfortably arranged in his arms, the telephone rang. She mumbled something and pulled the blanket over her head. He mumbled something a bit more pungent and lifted the receiver. "Hello?"

"Jack Slater?"

The gruff baritone on the other end of the line sounded vaguely familiar to Jack. He turned on the lamp and sat up. "Who's calling?"

"Hank Morosco. I'm a friend of Moe Kaplan's."

"Oh—yeah." Jack sat higher. "Yeah, thanks for getting back to me."

"I'm sorry it took me so long. I've made some inquiries, and no one knows anything about the stones in question. Nothing missing, nothing unaccounted for. No light shipments, nothing. My sense is, they simply don't exist. Do you know what I'm saying?"

"I think so."

"So keep your trap shut and count your blessings. You're a lucky man. Finders keepers, and all that."

"Right. Thanks."

"No problem. Give my best to Moe, would you? Tell him I'm going to mop the floor with him next time we play handball."

"I'll pass the word," Jack promised before hanging up.

Turning, he found Mandy wide-awake, gazing up at him with her breathtaking blue eyes. Staring into them made him wish for nothing more than to descend into her arms again. But his weary muscles protested, so he suppressed his baser urges and passed her the plate. "Sandwich?"

She took one and bit into it.

"Not as good as Nadine's roast, but it'll do," he said, helping himself to the other sandwich. "That phone call, in case you were wondering, was from a friend of Moe's. He works in the diamond district down in midtown."

"The diamond district," she repeated in a soft, inquisitive drawl. Her sensuous voice, combined with a glimpse of the creamy curve of her breast peeking above the edge of the blanket, was almost enough to make Jack lose his concentration.

"The heart of the diamond wholesale business. I gave him a call when I got back from Kentucky. I asked whether there was any industry scuttlebutt concerning missing diamonds."

She looked concerned. "I don't know that you should have discussed it with other people, Jack."

"I didn't want you running off to the authorities," he explained. "Not unless we knew what we were dealing with. Who knew? It could have been organized crime. It could have been a sting operation. Moe vouched for Hank Morosco, so I confided in him."

"What did he say?" Mandy asked before taking another dainty bite out of her sandwich.

"He explained that the usual way diamonds reach the United States is from South Africa, through the Netherlands. Purchases are sealed with a handshake. Millions of dollars in diamonds change hands without a written contract. It's a business based on trust."

"I see."

"So if someone had been ripped off, everyone would know about it. Word would have gotten out real fast."

She took another bite and chewed thoughtfully. "What-all does that have to do with the diamonds I got?"

"They're unaccounted for. No one knows where they came from or who has title to them. Which means, Mandy, that they're yours."

"But I have no proof, no papers—"

"Hanks says don't worry. You paid for the shipment, you even paid tax on it. It's yours."

"I reckon a fellow in Chinatown doesn't agree with that."

"Chinatown?"

"That's where Albert Stevenson operates. My quartz supplier."

"Forget him," Jack advised, washing down his sandwich with a swallow of wine. He drew Mandy into his lap and planted a kiss on the crown of her head. "Your supplier has nothing on you. He has no way of proving you got anything but rose-quartz crystals in that shipment, and he has no right to try to take the shipment away from you, not without going through legal channels. And he isn't going to hire a lawyer to represent him because then he'd have to reveal that he'd smuggled the diamonds."

"Not a lawyer, no. He's going to hire gorillas with guns. I don't want to live the rest of my life looking over my shoulder, Jack. What if Stevenson comes after me?"

"I'll make sure he doesn't."

"How?"

Good question. "Where are the diamonds now?" he asked.

"They're in a safe-deposit box."

"In Harrow?"

"No. They're well hidden, Jack. No one can get to them." She sighed and leaned back against Jack's chest. "So all that's left for now is getting the doll."

"The damned doll?" he quoted. "The stupid doll?"

"Moe Kaplan's doll. I know Moe now. Not as well as you do, but I've met him. I've seen his hands. I want him to have that doll."

"You said the crystals aren't going to cure his arthritis."

"I don't reckon I ever said that," she argued quietly. "What I said was, some people believe in them and maybe that's enough. I'd like to think it would be enough for Moe. I like him, Jack. I want to make him happy."

Jack closed his arms around her. He wanted to make her happy, too. And he suspected she wouldn't be happy until she had the doll back in her hands—or, more accurately, in Moe's. She had come all the way to New York, not knowing that Jack loved her, just to get the doll and return it to its rightful owner. It obviously meant a lot to her.

"We'll go together," he promised. "Tomorrow. We'll go to Chinatown and get this thing straightened out."

He felt her relax against him. Although he couldn't see her face, he could sense her smile. He could feel it warming his soul. Her faith in him was a strong, warm bond holding them together.

He would have promised her anything for this feeling of contentment. He would have promised her the sun, the moon, the stars and all the diamonds in heaven and on earth to have her love.

Unfortunately, he'd made the one promise he wasn't sure he could deliver on.

Damned if he knew how he was going to get the doll back.

Chapter Eleven

Had Jack actually thought traveling all the way to Harrow, Kentucky, in pursuit of the Moe doll was crazy? That jaunt seemed remarkably sane compared to what he and Mandy were contemplating as they munched on toasted English muffins and sipped coffee in the sun-filled dining alcove of his apartment.

"Forget about a bodyguard, Jack," she said. "I don't rightly see the need for one. At least, not until we know for sure that there's a genuine danger."

"What would you call having your car forced over a cliff and a gun shoved into your neck? An *ungen-uine* danger?"

Sighing, she stirred a teaspoon of sugar into her coffee, her crystalline blue eyes focused on a point in the distance through the window. It dawned on Jack that this was the first time he and Mandy had ever had breakfast together. Until that moment he hadn't known she took sugar in her coffee.

"You didn't happen to bring your rifle with you?" he half asked, then corrected himself. "Your shotgun, I mean."

"I didn't reckon they'd let me carry it onto the plane. Airlines are funny that way." She tapped her spoon against the edge of her mug to shake off the excess coffee. Jack took note of every detail, every trivial gesture. He watched the way she used both hands to lift the mug, the way she pursed her lips and blew on the steamy beverage before she tasted it. "Do you have a gun?" she asked.

"*Me?* This is Manhattan, lady. We don't shoot squirrels for supper around here. The only people who own guns are cops and criminals."

She frowned, deep in thought.

"I've got my pocketknife," he reminded her. "Lucky for me, Bill McIntyre didn't tag it and lock it in the evidence room." He popped the last of his muffin into his mouth and swallowed. "So, given that neither of us is armed to the teeth, what's your objection to hiring a bodyguard?"

Mandy opened her mouth and then shut it, allowing herself more time to consider her answer. "The notion just doesn't set right with me, Jack. Where I come from, folks fight their own battles."

"Of course. Like the Hatfields and the McCoys."

Mandy responded to his teasing by crumpling her napkin and throwing it at him. Then she grew serious. "This is our quarrel with Albert Stevenson. I believe we ought to deal with it ourselves."

Cripes, he thought, she was more macho than he was. "Let me remind you, Mandy, that you were the one who said a bunch of diamonds wasn't worth risking our lives over."

"The diamonds aren't what's important here," she argued. "They're perfectly safe, and miles from New York. And anyway, your friend from the diamond business seems to think they're mine, fair and square."

"Uh-huh. That's what we'll say to Albert Stevenson as he's stringing us up by our feet. 'The diamonds are Mandy's, fair and square. So please don't flog us too hard.'"

"He's not going to flog us," Mandy declared.

"You're right. He'll probably just search our pockets and then shoot us, a single discreet bullet to the base of the skull. That's how the pros do it, you know." He took a long, bracing drink of coffee and put down his mug with a resolute thump. "I don't know about you, Mandy, but I'd rather part with five hundred bucks for a bodyguard than have my vital systems permanently disconnected."

"Five hundred dollars? Is that how much a bodyguard will cost?"

"I have no idea how much they cost. Before I met you, I never needed to hire one." He went into the kitchen for the telephone directory and carried it back to the table.

Mandy's eyes widened when she saw how thick the book was. "Is that for the entire state, or just the city?"

"Just the borough of Manhattan. One-fifth of the city." He flipped the directory open to the Yellow Pages and scanned the contents in search of security services.

"Jack..." Her sultry drawl massaged some subconscious part of his soul, even while his conscious mind was focused on the task of scouring the directory listings. "Jack, if you truly think I'm endangering you, I'll do this alone. Getting the doll back is my responsibility."

Merely listening to the low, enticing purr of her voice made him want to invite her to endanger him all she wanted. "We're in this together, Mandy," he said, pleased that his words didn't betray the arousal that continued to simmer inside him whenever she spoke, whenever he caught a glimpse of her, whenever he thought about his big, comfy bed down the hall and the indescribable enjoyment he'd had sharing it with her throughout the night. "Let me make a few calls and see what I can work out."

Using his finger to hold his place in the directory, he stood once more and headed for the telephone in the kitchen. Passing by her chair, he leaned over and placed a light kiss on her forehead. Her hair smelled dark and sweet, like the mossy forests of eastern Kentucky.

The hell with the doll, he almost blurted out. *Let's go back to bed. Let's make love for the rest of the day.*

Yet one of the things about her that turned him on was her willingness to risk life and limb, not for a doll or diamonds, but for a principle, for Moe and the magic of the rose-quartz crystals. This wasn't about protecting her windfall wealth or proving her mettle. It was about taking responsibility and taking chances, about honor and courage and...well, doing something crazy.

Falling in love was crazy. Since Jack had already done something crazy with this woman, he might as well go the distance.

WHEN SHE HAD GONE after Albert Stevenson yesterday, she'd been apprehensive.

Today, however, as she and Jack strolled down Mott Street, her hand tucked securely inside his, she didn't feel the least bit afraid.

One thing had changed since yesterday: today she had Jack. Not just had him sauntering along the sidewalk next to her, but had him in her heart, in her soul, as much as it was possible to have a man such as him.

That, more than anything, gave her the courage to face Albert Stevenson.

After one rent-a-cop agency offered to send a bodyguard that morning, no questions asked—for ten thousand dollars—they'd decided to forego that route.

"What we'll do," Jack resolved once he'd hung up the phone, "is reconnoiter."

"What do you mean?"

"We'll mosey on down to Chinatown and discreetly check out the situation. If we get a bad feeling about it, we'll make a quick retreat and rethink our strategy.''

They'd taken the subway downtown, an adventure in itself. Unlike her cab ride from the airport, the subway tore through its underground tunnels without her having to witness near collisions with other vehicles. Lights flashed like strobes through the windows, and she and Jack rocked and jounced as they clung to the vertical pole in the center of the car and tried to maintain their balance. At one point, when the lights flickered off inside the car, Jack closed his hands protectively over hers. It was a small deed, something he probably hadn't even thought about, yet she was touched by his concern.

Now they were out in the open again, in the sharp shadows of the buildings that crowded out the morning sun. "Chinatown," Jack affirmed happily as they waited for a Don't Walk light to change. "I haven't been down this way in ages. We ought to have lunch here.''

Mandy eyed the grocery shop with the smoked fowl hanging in the window and felt her throat choke shut. "We just had breakfast.''

"At least we ought to buy some lichee nuts for a snack. Have you ever had lichee nuts?''

"No. And to tell the truth, I don't feel the least bit deprived.''

The light read Walk and they crossed the street. "This is his block," Mandy murmured as they stepped up onto the sidewalk at the opposite corner.

Jack slowed his pace and surveyed the street. "Which building?" he asked.

"The one above the shoe-repair shop."

As if on cue, the door of Albert Stevenson's building opened and out stepped a tiny elderly woman lugging a bulky, bulging tote bag.

"That's her."

"Who?"

"The lady who answered the door yesterday. She told me to forget about the doll and go away."

"Wasn't that helpful of her," Jack muttered, his dark gaze riveted to the woman as she descended the steps to the street and turned right. Maintaining a cautious distance, he and Mandy stalked her. "I wonder what's in her bag."

"Do you think the doll's in there?"

"Who knows? Maybe the doll, maybe a few pounds of uncut diamonds. Maybe a body."

"What are we going to do?" she whispered.

"Trail her for a while, see what she does."

She crossed the street. They waited until she was halfway down the next block before they crossed. Jack tugged Mandy's hand to stop her when the woman descended a few steps to a below-ground-level door and went inside. When she emerged, she was empty-handed.

"The drop," Jack announced ponderously.

"What drop?"

"You want to wait outside or come in with me?" he asked, resuming his leisurely pace down the street.

"I'll come in," she said. Even if it meant walking into an ambush, she didn't want Jack to walk through that door without her.

They reached the short flight of steps down to a basement storefront. Beneath some Chinese figures, the words Chou's Dry Cleaners—Tailoring were painted on the glass in bright red. "I'll do the talking," Jack alerted her before letting go of her hand and proceeding down the stairs. Mandy recited a brief prayer under her breath and followed him down.

He strode into the store, pulling his wallet out of his hip pocket as he approached the young man standing behind the counter. Jack flipped his wallet open, shut it with brisk efficiency and stuffed it back into his pocket. "Charlie McCarthy from the FBI," he said. "I'd like to see that bag that was just delivered here."

The man behind the counter appeared suitably daunted. "You want to see her laundry?"

Jack nodded. "It's part of an ongoing investigation."

"Here." The man lifted the elderly woman's bag onto the counter.

Jack rummaged through its contents and nodded solemnly. "Hmm. Interesting. Thank you, sir. I appreciate your cooperation." He touched his index finger to his forehead in a casual salute, then pivoted and marched to the door. Mandy hurried out after him.

They were halfway down the street before she dared to speak. "Charlie McCarthy?"

"It was the first name that came to my mind."

"*Charlie McCarthy?* He was a dummy!"

"The symbolism of that boggles my mind," Jack muttered. "Lucky for me I didn't think of Mortimer Snerd first."

"What was in the bag?"

"Dirty laundry. Shirts, mostly. Very large shirts."

Mandy recalled the very large man she'd glimpsed in silhouette yesterday when she'd been perched on the fire escape outside Albert Stevenson's building. "No doll, huh?"

"No doll. No diamonds. Nothing of value to anyone other than a man with an eighteen-inch neck."

They had returned to the block where Mandy had first encountered the elderly woman in apartment 3-B. "What do we do now?"

"Reconnoiter some more," Jack said, backing toward the curb and tilting his head back to view the entire building. "Which window do you think is his?"

"Third floor," Mandy said, counting up. "I'd guess those two, on the left."

"I wonder why his shades are closed in at ten in the morning."

"He could be napping. Maybe we shouldn't disturb him."

"Maybe this is the best time to disturb him," Jack remarked, shading his eyes with his hand as the morning sun glared over the flat roofline.

The sound of car doors slamming behind her drew her attention from the building to the street. Two police cars had double-parked in front of the building, and four uniformed officers rushed toward the building. "Jack, look!"

"Don't stare," he whispered. "We don't want them to think we're part of this."

Part of what? she wondered, watching as the officers hustled up the stairs and vanished into the building. "Do you think they're going to arrest him?" she asked Jack.

"For what? A fatal case of ring-around-the-collar?" Jack glanced up at 3-B's windows and shook his head. "I wish there were some way we could see what was going on without getting in the middle of it."

"There's a fire escape out back," Mandy told him.

Jack's face lit up. "Let's go."

Mandy led the way around the building to the garbage-strewn alley. The ladder she'd used yesterday to climb down from the fire escape was cranked and secured in place on the metal platform one story up. "We can't get up there," she lamented.

"Sure we can." In a swift, agile motion, Jack tucked his head between her legs and hoisted her up on his shoulders. He stood sturdily beneath her, awing her with his strength. She knew she wasn't all that light, but he didn't seem to be straining at all.

In herself she did feel a strain, but it had nothing to do with being lifted. It had to do with the warmth of his hands on her thighs, the heat of his neck against her crotch. A sudden surge of longing overtook her.

She stared at the rusty metal piping of the fire escape and hoped the sensation would fade. Now was definitely not the appropriate time to feel what she was feeling, to want what she was wanting.

She had to stretch to reach the bottom bar. As soon as she had a good grip on it, Jack cupped his hands under her feet and heaved her the rest of the way up. She eased the ladder down for him slowly, trying to keep the mechanism from making any noise.

They quickly scaled the ladder to the second floor, and then to the third. Peeking furtively through the window, they were able to see the four police officers crowded around the door to 3-B. "They've found him out," Mandy cheered.

"Found what out? Don't be so happy. He might tell them *you're* the one who's got the diamonds."

"What diamonds?" she said smugly. "Your jeweler friend said no one knows they're missing. And no one can prove I have them. They're nowhere near my house."

"I can't believe you're the same person who wanted to turn them over to the authorities and pretend you'd never seen them," Jack needled her.

It was true. Just days ago, she'd considered the diamonds the bane of her existence. They'd brought her brother injury—although that injury had in turn brought him a rather friendly truce with his ex-wife. The diamonds had brought Mandy face-to-face with her own mortality—but she'd survived. They'd brought her the misery of falling in love with Jack—and the bliss of being in love with him.

Whatever torment she'd suffered had toughened her, emboldened her. She had Jack, she had the diamonds, and she was about to have the sublime pleasure of watching the police dispose of the one person who posed a threat to her safety. All that was missing was the doll.

Through the thick glass of the window they heard a muffled bang as one of the officers kicked in the door. The bang was followed by shouting, pounding, the whistle and pop of a gun firing—and Jack cursing. A blur of bodies tumbled into the hallway, a tangle of arms and legs scuffling and shouting, making their clumsy way toward the window.

"Run!" Jack shouted, shoving her toward the ladder.

She scampered down, missing a rung and letting out a yelp, stumbling her way onto the second-floor platform. Jack was inches behind her. The entire metal structure trembled; voices hollered from an open window.

"Keep going!" Jack ordered her, pushing her off the bottom ladder when she was still several feet above the ground.

She landed with a bone-jarring thud—and kept going.

She heard footsteps at her back, odd noises rebounding against the narrow walls of the alley, the sounds of people stomping and crunching through the trash. She heard shouts, grunts, panting. She dared to glance over her shoulder and found Jack vaulting at her, propelling her around the corner of a building and slamming her into a wall. Pain seared through her knees, her hands, her chest as he pressed her into the unyielding brick, smothering her.

"Jack!" She thought she'd screamed it, but she could scarcely hear her own voice. Her lungs were compressed, her head light from the absence of air.

Gradually he relented, his hands growing gentle on her shoulders and his lips grazing the crown of her head. He took a step back and she crumpled backward against him.

"Are you okay?" he asked. "Mandy... Oh, God, I hurt you. I'm sorry." He slid his hands up and down her arms, then wrapped them around her, letting her rest against him.

She sucked in deep, desperate lungfuls of air. "Why did you do that?" she asked, her voice feeble and shaky.

"Didn't you hear the gun?"

"Inside the building, you mean?"

"Right behind us. Someone—one of the cops and someone else, a great big monster of a guy—came down into the alley. They were fighting. I heard a gun go off, and..." He turned her in his arms and crushed his lips to hers.

She'd just begun to regain her equilibrium, but the ferocious power of his kiss undid her. Her already sore knees turned gelatinous and she clung to him, partly because she didn't want to collapse and partly because she wanted him to keep kissing her. She wanted him more than she had when he'd heaved her onto his shoulders. More than when she'd awakened beside him in his bed that morning.

Someone had fired a gun in an alley. Someone behind them. Albert Stevenson, the policeman, it didn't matter. They'd nearly died.

They were alive, and she never wanted to stop kissing Jack.

He was apparently ready to stop, however. Pulling back, he gazed around him at the high walls surrounding them, the distant patch of blue sky above them. She looked around, too, and realized that they were in a different alley, one that must have branched off from the first.

"Did they see us?"

"I don't know how they could have avoided seeing us."

"Where are they now?"

Jack stole quietly toward the entry to the alley. Pressing his back against the wall, he peered around the bend. He let out a long breath, then waved for Mandy to join him.

Her legs still felt rubbery. As her passion faded, it left behind a vacuum that was quickly filled with fear.

Guns. Alleys. The big man, Stevenson, had seen her and Jack. She began to wonder whether ten thousand dollars for a bodyguard might have been a bargain.

"Let's get out of here," Jack said, whisking her through the maze of alleys to the street.

In the sunlight she paused and inspected herself for damage. Her palms had tiny pebbles imbedded in them; her jeans were caked with dust. Her knees were stiff and aching.

"I did hurt you," Jack said contritely. "Mandy, I'm sorry, I only meant—"

"It's all right."

"They were so close behind us. And there was a gun. All I wanted was—"

"It's all right," she insisted, ringing her arms around his waist and resting her face against his shoulder, seeking reassurance as she gave it. The solid feel of him consoled her. Once again he had saved her life—a bit roughly, perhaps, but better bruised knees than a bullet in her back.

He returned her embrace, one arm spanning her waist and holding her close, the other hand sliding up under her hair to guide her lips to his. This kiss was less brutal than the one in the alley, but just as passionate. A pedestrian strolling by hooted and whistled at them; another clicked her tongue in condemnation.

Mandy didn't care that she and Jack were making a spectacle of themselves. All she cared about was having his loving arms around her.

Abruptly he stiffened. "Son of a gun," he muttered, easing back and staring past her. She traced the angle of his glowering gaze and saw a familiar face.

One of the thugs.

A throng had gathered at the foot of the steps by the shoe-repair shop, gawking as a police officer marched two handcuffed men out of the building. Neither of them was particularly huge. One she'd never seen before. The other she'd seen in her house in Harrow, in her cellar and her yard. She'd seen him in a rain-soaked parking lot outside Canaan Community Hospital. She'd seen him holding a gun to her throat.

"It's him!" she cried.

Jack clamped his hand over her mouth, but not fast enough. The handcuffed thug glanced her way—and so did one of the gawkers.

The other thug.

Among the disadvantages of having long, curly, fire red hair was that one couldn't easily fade into a crowd. Mandy and the second thug had seen each other only one time, when he and the creep with the gun had barreled through her house and stolen Jack's doll. Yet as vividly as she remembered him, he remembered her.

He hadn't hurt her, she tried to remind herself. As best she could figure, he'd been the one who had been busy pumping Bill McIntyre full of liquor while his sidekick went after Jessie. The first guy—the one with the manacled wrists being escorted down the stairs and into a waiting police cruiser—was the dangerous one. This fellow had simply been assisting.

He was still free, standing anonymously amid the throng of rubberneckers watching the arrest from the sidewalk.

She wanted to turn and flee, but Jack held her in place. To her utter amazement, the thug turned and fled instead.

Instinct overtook her. She broke away from Jack's restraining grip and charged after the man.

He reached the corner and darted heedlessly into the traffic. Ignoring the residual soreness in her knees, she chased him into the street. A car screeched to a stop so close to her she could feel the heat of its engine. She heard Jack yell something but she kept running.

The thug might have thought he'd escaped the police. But he hadn't escaped Mandy. He sprinted down the sidewalk, forcing a bicycle rider off balance and provoking a hail of expletives from him. Mandy flashed an apologetic smile as she raced past the cyclist.

The thug was a fast runner, and it took all her effort not to lose him. Her lungs burned, her leg muscles cramped and her sides developed more stitches than a patchwork quilt. But she couldn't let up. She couldn't let him get away.

Behind her she heard swift footsteps. Jack's shadow nipped at her heels, then slid under her feet as he gained on her. Pulling up next to her, he said, "Take it easy, Mandy—I'll get him," then forged ahead.

The hell with that. Jack wasn't going to do it all. She was going to be there with him, no matter how it ended. Either they'd win together or they'd lose together.

Summoning what little energy she had left, she pressed on, struggling not to fall too far behind.

A block ahead, the thug turned the corner. Five precious seconds later, Jack reached the corner and veered right, disappearing around the edge of a building. Three more seconds and she made the turn.

They were gone.

Arms akimbo, she gasped for breath and searched the street. The nearest buildings appeared to be warehouses or factories of some sort, forbidding gray edifices lacking windows and doors. A couple of them had fire escapes abutting the front facades, but Mandy saw nobody climbing them, nobody leaping from roof to roof.

Scowling, she combed the street with her gaze. An eighteen-wheeler rumbled past, its springs whining and the rear door rattling in its joints. When it finally passed her, she noticed a driveway that led directly into a building, into a yawning blackness.

Throwing back her shoulders in a posture of courage, she crossed the street and approached the driveway. It opened into an underground garage.

Mandy told herself she was slowing down only because she was exhausted, but the truth was, dread was finally settling in and taking hold. As she ventured down the dark, spooky ramp into the echoing concrete cave, a surge of panic washed through her, leaving her queasy.

What if this was a trap? What if he had deliberately lured her and Jack into this dark, eerie hall of echoes for some gruesome end? What if Jack had already reached that end?

Rather than repel her, the possibility only made her pick up her pace. If Jack was in trouble, if he was hurt, she had to be with him, no matter what the cost to herself.

By the time she'd left the ramp for the first parking level her eyes had adjusted to the gloom. Scrutinizing the cars parked in rows so tight and neat they reminded her of planted crops, she listened for the sound of people moving about. She heard an engine ignite. The motor echoed deafeningly against the steel-and-cement walls.

She sidled along a narrow aisle and pressed up against a wall as the car coasted past her. When at last the distorted rumble faded with the car gliding up the ramp to the street, she heard something else, something quieter, like the scrabbling of a mouse across a kitchen floor.

Or the scrabbling of two men across the concrete.

She began running again.

"Don't!" came a strangled voice. "Don't hurt me!"

Oh, God. *Jack,* she whispered to herself, *hang on. I'm coming.* As if she had half a chance in hell of being able to save him.

She swung around a thick cement support column and saw motion, a dark arm swooping down, another dark figure tumbling to the floor.

"Don't hurt me!" came the strangled voice again.

Now she was close enough to recognize that it wasn't Jack's voice. Relief billowed through her as she loped between two rows of cars to where Jack hovered over the thug, who lay supine on the cold gray floor. Jack had his knee planted firmly at the center of the thug's chest. His hands were wrapped around the thug's neck.

"Don't kill him, Jack," she advised.

Jack glanced up at her. He wasn't even breathing hard, while she was still wheezing from her run. Her hair was a mess of snarls and frizz, while he looked completely unruffled. His jacket was on straight, his jeans barely wrinkled. His dark eyes glittered with an odd combination of anger and glee.

"After what his buddy did to your brother," he said, "the least I ought to do is break his jaw."

"Why don't we just turn him over to the police?" she suggested.

The man on the floor looked frantic. "I'd rather you break my jaw," he said in that strange, clogged voice.

Jack turned back to him. He relaxed his thumbs slightly against the man's windpipe, although he kept his hands in place. "Who are you?" he asked.

"Albert Stevenson."

"You are not," Mandy retorted. Albert Stevenson was the giant with the dirty size-eighteen shirts. "If you lie," she threatened, "I reckon we'll just take you on down to the police."

"I swear, I'm not lying," he protested. "I swear it. Look—just let me go and I'll be gone. You'll never hear from me again. The diamonds are yours."

"What diamonds?" she said cagily. Jack's mouth skewed upward in a fleeting smile of approval at her feigned ignorance.

The thug nodded as best he could, what with Jack's hands still circling his neck and the chilly floor under his head. "Right. What diamonds?"

"Who are you?" she questioned him. Jack had the man completely immobile. Mandy decided an interrogation was in order.

"I told you. I'm Albert Stevenson."

"Who's the elderly lady?"

"His wife."

"*Whose* wife?"

"Your supplier's."

She scowled. Jack moved his thumbs experimentally over the man's throat, generating a peculiar gurgling sound from him. "Albert Stevenson is my supplier," she said.

"No," the man argued, eyeing Jack with alarm. "*I'm* Albert Stevenson. The big guy was just using my name to bring in the diamonds. The diamonds that don't exist," he added, shooting Jack another chary look.

"The big guy? Who's the big guy?"

"Felix Crimmins."

"Felix Crimmins?" Mandy's scowl intensified; she felt the muscles cramping along her brow. "Felix

Crimmins was my old supplier. He retired. He's been sick for some time now, in and out of the hospital. The last time I called him, his wife told me . . ."

"Yeah. That's his wife. The old lady."

Stunned, Mandy sank onto the hard concrete and leaned back against the support column. Felix Crimmins was a sweet, elderly man, wasn't he? He'd supplied her with rose-quartz crystals for three years, until he'd become ill and given her the name of another supplier: Albert Stevenson.

"Listen," she said, refusing to accept this stranger's story. "I never had a moment's grief with Felix Crimmins. He shipped me my quartz and I paid him, and everything was just fine and dandy. Nobody ever ransacked my house or beat up my brother."

"Or threatened to shoot you," Jack added, flexing his thumbs and causing Albert Stevenson to flinch in sheer terror.

"That was Ray's idea, not mine. I was off singing 'Bottle of Wine' with that cracker cop you got down there in Kentucky. Ray's a hothead. I never woulda done that number on you."

Jack glanced at Mandy. She reckoned she looked as dubious as he did. "Why," she asked Stevenson, "would Felix Crimmins suddenly have decided to send me diamonds?"

"It was a mess," the man on the floor explained. "I told him not to do it, but when you're arguing with a guy that stands six foot eight and tips the scales at two-seventy, you don't argue too hard. He had to take the diamonds in payment from some hombre down in Rio. The guy had a cash-flow problem or some such. I says to Felix, I says, don't take diamonds. You're just asking for trouble.''

"What was Felix Crimmins being paid for?" Mandy asked.

"Guns," Stevenson groaned. "What do you think the cops were busting him for this morning?"

"Guns?" Mandy and Jack exclaimed in unison.

"What do you think, Felix made a living by selling worthless stones?"

"They aren't worthless," Mandy snapped. "Rose-quartz crystals make people's wishes come true."

"Yeah," Stevenson grunted. "And my mother's the queen of England. Didn't you know Felix's main operation was gun sales? Import, export, under the table, untraceable. The crystals were just a cover. That's why he mixed the diamonds in with the stones." He paused to swallow, which was apparently hard to do with Jack's hands around his throat. "We were supposed to get the package back once it was in the States. He shipped it to you—" he twisted his head toward Mandy "—on account of Kentucky was his closest client. He used my name, so it wouldn't be traceable back to him. Then he sent me and Ray down to pick up the shipment. I guess we didn't do so hot."

"You did hot enough," Jack muttered. "You stole my doll."

"Oh, yeah. The doll. I says to Ray, let's take the doll and run, but he says, no, we gotta get the rest of the stones. He's a hothead, you know?"

"We know." Jack nodded. "So, where's the doll?"

"You don't want the doll."

"Yes, I do."

"It's not in such hot shape."

"Listen, pal—you use the word hot one more time, and my temper's going to catch fire. Now, let me just make sure I've got it straight. That raid this morning was about gun smuggling?"

"Yeah."

"And the big guy was arrested?"

"I understand it took them a while to subdue him out in the back alley. They got Ray and Bernie Mingus. The old lady, I don't know where she went off to. They'll get her, though. Ray and Bernie won't protect her."

"Will they protect you?"

"You kiddin'? If you ever take your thumbs off my neck, I'm outta here. New name, new city. Nobody's ever gonna hear of Albert Stevenson again."

"Okay." Jack thought for a moment, then loosened his hands. He kept his knee on Stevenson's chest, though. "I still want my doll."

"You want it? It's yours. Let me get it, it's in my car. And, hey, listen, I understand about your knifing my tires. No hard feelings."

"Yeah? Well, I've got hard feelings. You should have seen what I went through with the insurance company when I reported my rental car went over a cliff.''

"Well, hey, no hard feelings, okay? I'll get you your doll, and you'll forget you ever met me.''

"I'll never forget," Jack muttered. He carefully lifted his knee from Stevenson's chest, and at the same time slid his arm around Stevenson's neck. With his free hand, he pinned Stevenson's arm behind him. "Let's go to your car and get the doll.''

"Okay," Stevenson said meekly. "Sure thing. Just—hey, remember, what happened to the doll, Ray did it. Ray and the big guy.''

"Right. It's all their fault. A thousand curses on their heads. Now where's your car?''

Shackled by Jack's imprisoning grip on him, Albert Stevenson moved awkwardly along a row of cars.

Mandy felt dazed. If Stevenson was telling the truth, the diamonds actually belonged to her. No one would find them, no one would claim them.

She was rich. Unbelievably rich.

Unless, of course, something went wrong. Maybe Stevenson's car was booby-trapped. Maybe the instant he and Jack got there, events would take an appalling turn.

Swallowing, she trailed Jack and his captive past aisle after aisle of cars, down another ramp and deep into the bowels of the garage. The dim overhead bulbs leaked a jaundiced light into the air.

I love Jack, she murmured to herself in prayer. *That's all that matters—that I love him. That we get out of this thing alive. If Jack returns my love, I'm as rich as I'll ever want to be. Just let us survive.*

She recognized the sedan beside which Jack and Stevenson drew to a halt, right down to the splatters of dried Kentucky mud on its fenders. She watched as Stevenson unlocked a door, pulled it as far open as he could, and groped for something on the floor. A gun she thought.

She squeezed her eyes shut, unable to bear watching. *Oh, no, Jack...*

"Oh, jeez," Jack groaned.

She forced herself to look. He was holding a limp, flat, tattered lump of cloth.

"I'm sorry," Stevenson said. "They wanted what was inside it. I guess they coulda been neater."

Jack looked enraged. As Mandy neared him, her anger expanded to match his. The doll she'd handcrafted had been scissored open from its neck to its belly. One of its feet was missing. Its head had been skewered enough times to reveal that it was stuffed with foam, not stones.

Jack spun around and lunged at Stevenson, knocking him back into his car. "I ought to kill you for this!"

"Jack, don't! Let's just go."

He was breathing hard as she pried him off Stevenson and pulled him back. He shook the demolished doll at Stevenson, who raised his arms protectively in front of him. "I wanted this doll!"

Jack roared. "I've been fighting for this doll for days now."

"I'm sorry, man! I'm sorry!"

Mandy clamped her hand around Jack's upper arm. She felt the hard bulge of his biceps through his jacket and shirt. She felt the tension in him, the bitter fury.

For God's sake, she thought, they were alive. Her diamonds were safe. She had all the money in the world to make a new doll for Moe. What on earth was wrong with Jack?

She let her hand fall from him. As they walked side by side up the ramp and across the next level, moving wearily, mutely, inexorably toward the daylight, she knew.

Mandy loved him and she wanted a lifetime with him. But when all was said and done, the only thing Jack had ever really wanted wasn't even the doll—it was the diamonds.

Chapter Twelve

He and Mandy were safe. The bad guys no longer posed a threat. Nothing stood in the way of their happiness.

Then why did everything feel wrong all of a sudden?

As the taxi carried them uptown, Jack continued to seethe. On his lap sat the doll, frayed and flat, its threads unraveling from its multiple wounds. Beside him, Mandy gazed out the window, obviously in a sour mood.

Mandy sighed.

"What?" Jack asked.

"I said I'd make you a new doll," she snapped, as if his question had turned on a switch inside her. "But all you can do is sulk. Moe wouldn't care if he got a new doll, but you would. You'd be out your diamonds. If that's really all that matters to you—"

Jack shot a quick glance toward the driver. If he'd heard Mandy mention diamonds, he didn't show it. "I don't want your diamonds," he said in a low voice.

"I understand it's my fault," she continued as if she hadn't heard him. "You lost your doll trying to help me. So, really, Jack, there's nothing I'd rather do than run up a new doll on the machine, and then take some diamonds and . . . and *stuff* them."

Probably up some part of his anatomy, Jack thought.

"There's really nothing to it," she continued, her eyes glinting like the blue centers of twin flames. "I'll just—"

"All right." His voice was icy, and it froze her just as he'd hoped. "What exactly is your problem, lady?"

"My problem—" she sounded less righteous now, more tormented "—is that for you, all this has ever been about is the damned diamonds. The only special thing about this doll is that it once had diamonds in it. Well, it doesn't anymore. So forget it."

"Forget it? No, Mandy. I want this doll. I love this doll. I've gone through hell and high water for this doll. Maybe the fact that it's ruined means nothing to you, but it means something to me."

"Because it used to be stuffed with a fortune."

"Because it brought us together."

Mandy fell silent.

Jack was embarrassed to reveal his sentimental streak, but it was the truth. *This* doll had brought him to Mandy, had made him want to lay down his life for her. Another doll would be just a replacement, not the original one. This was the one with the magic.

Although it seemed now as if the magic had been emptied out of it along with the diamonds.

Mandy blinked away a tear. "I reckon it did bring us together," she agreed, her tone soft and tremulous. "But it can't keep us together."

"What can?"

She gazed up at him, and when another tear leaked past the coppery fringe of her lashes, she let it skitter down her cheek. "Diamonds?"

He used his thumb to catch the teardrop and wipe it away. "God, no."

"You really don't want them?"

"What the hell would I do with them? I'm not the jewelry type." He smiled slightly, and Mandy's responding smile looked awfully teary. "No, I don't want them, Mandy. All I want is you."

"And a doll."

"This doll." He picked it up and studied it. "Any chance you can fix it?"

Mandy took it from him. "I suppose I could try."

"That's all I want."

"And me?"

He arched his arm around her and brushed her lips with his. "And you."

THE THOUGHT of returning to Harrow alone depressed her, but there was no way around it.

"I can't come with you," Jack explained as they lay naked in his bed that evening, the top sheet lying in steamy wrinkles over their bodies, his chest cushioning her head and his arm wrapped snugly around her. He toyed with a springy curl of her hair and slid his knee gently along the inside of her thigh. "The business can't run without me. If it could, I'd fire myself."

"I understand," she said dolefully. But her thoughts wandered to her empty house, her workbench, her CDs. And her big lonely bed.

"I still don't see why you can't stay here in New York with me."

"I've got orders to fill."

"Big deal. If your other clients really wanted their orders, they would have gone to Harrow like I did."

Mandy smiled in spite of herself. "They didn't go to Harrow because they're normal, rational folks. That doesn't mean I don't have to fill their orders. And besides, you want me to fix your doll, don't you?"

"So bring what you need to New York. We can buy you a sewing machine and fabric, and—"

"Jack." He certainly had no qualms about going after what he wanted, even if it was totally illogical or impractical.

He lifted her onto him and cupped his hands around her face, angling it so he could stare into her eyes. She ran her finger along the rough surface of his unshaven jaw.

"I'm not real good at making romantic speeches, but..." He took a deep breath. "I want you in my life. I hope you know that."

"I'm in your life, Jack," she vowed, startled by the sudden sting of tears in her eyes.

His eyes were dry, but they gazed up into her face with a penetrating force, locking her attention and seizing her soul. "I don't want to sound jealous or possessive or anything, but . . ."

"But . . . ?"

"But I guess I *am* jealous, a little. I think of you with Bobby Lee, and—"

"That's history, Jack. Old history."

"And Robert E. Lee lost the war," Jack reminded himself with a wry grin. Then he grew solemn again. "I don't ever want to think of you with him, or with anyone else. I want it to be just you and me. I want to be the only man in your life, Mandy."

"What you want is what you've got."

"I love you," he whispered.

"I love you, too." Maybe he wasn't good at making romantic speeches—but neither was she. She wasn't the sort of person who used the word love casually or cavalierly. She couldn't recall actually admitting aloud that she loved Bobby Lee, even when they were living together and discussing marriage.

She hadn't known Jack anywhere near as long as she'd known Bobby Lee. She didn't know Jack anywhere near as well. But she knew certain things. They owed each other their lives. They were allies. They could face any enemy together. She could depend on Jack to protect her—even if he had to bruise her knees in the process—and she could count on him to honor the responsibilities as well as the joys of love. And she knew he felt things as deeply as she did.

"I wish I didn't have to go back to Harrow," she said, then sighed. "But I've got my job to do, just like you've got yours. Whichever one of us catches up on our work first can visit the other one."

"I never catch up," he complained, tilting his head so she could trail her fingers all the way to his ear. "The minute I think things are settled, a bunch of new contracts comes in."

"And the minute I think I've finished my orders, a bunch of new orders comes in," she countered, aware of the changes in his body under hers, the flexing of his abdominal muscles, the strategic shifting of his legs. A hushed sigh escaped her as something flowered open inside her, a slow, lush blossoming of damp sensation as her body answered his.

"It's a drag, isn't it?" he murmured huskily, moving his hands languidly up and down her back, along her sides, forward to her breasts. "We're too devoted to our careers, Mandy. We're going to have to figure something out."

"Not right this minute," she whispered, arching her back as he stroked her breasts. When he captured her mouth with his she heard herself moan, heard the demands of her heart as he found her, filled her, awakened her to the full understanding of how wonderful it was to be with him, and how agonizing it would be to leave him.

But leave him she did.

IT WASN'T UNTIL she arrived at her remote mountainside house that the first traces of uneasiness fluttered awake inside her. The house looked fine. The new lock she'd installed on the front door before she'd left for New York had held out any intruders who might have come along. The interior was exactly as she'd left it.

Even so, something was wrong. She examined the stack of letters she'd found in her mailbox one more time and scowled.

Bobby Lee had told her he would place her diamonds in a safe-deposit box and mail her the key. But none of her mail was from him.

All right. The postal system had its off days. Surely the key was on its way. She had no reason to worry about it.

Still, a vague premonition of trouble niggled at her.

She didn't let on when Jack telephoned her that night. He was the best thing in her life; she saw no need to bother him with what she was certain were groundless doubts.

"I miss you" were Jack's first words.

Dear Lord, how could she have ever thought he was after her diamonds? "I miss you, too," she confessed.

He asked her about her flight, made a few accurate wisecracks about airline food, inquired as to Jessie's convalescence. And then, "I can't come down this weekend—I've got to work Saturday and maybe Sunday, too, just catching up. But next weekend, if you'd like, I could fly down and see you."

"If I'd like? I'd love it!"

"I'll be with you as soon as I can get away," he promised. "Dream of me tonight."

"I will," she promised, although she doubted she'd be able to fall asleep without him beside her.

She did sleep, and she did dream: of Chinatown, of threading her sewing machine, of Iris pureeing food in a blender for Jessie. Of diamonds. A drawstring sack filled with them. A night sky speckled with diamonds instead of stars.

And an empty safe-deposit box.

She awakened the next morning feeling poorly rested and inexplicably uneasy. As she prepared a pot of coffee, she wrestled with the nasty aftertaste of her dream, that resounding image of an overly air-conditioned windowless room at a bank, a table, a long, rectangular steel drawer inexplicably empty.

It was a ridiculous image. A few cups of coffee and some productive work on her dolls would chase it away.

That, plus the afternoon mail, which would surely have the safe-deposit box key in it.

But the postal carrier left only two envelopes for her: a bill and a newsy letter from her parents.

Surely she couldn't have expected Bobby Lee to drop everything the instant he'd received her diamonds. He might have set them aside for a day or two, figuring he'd see to them when it was convenient for him. Of course, if he'd opened the sack and taken a peek at its contents, he would have rushed straight out to the bank and locked the diamonds away.

Or, a suspicious voice inside her nagged, he would have absconded with them.

Don't be silly, she admonished herself. Bobby Lee Nash was a gentleman, a man of honor. He was a proud son of the South. He would never steal Mandy's diamonds.

Any day now the key would arrive.

BUT IT DIDN'T. As the days slipped by without a word from Bobby Lee, what had once been a tiny, niggling anxiety had swelled into a gigantic, bellowing anxiety. She telephoned his apartment, but no one answered. The sound of his phone ringing and ringing on the other end of the line grated on her nerves. Finally, at Bobby Lee's private office number, a secretary answered.

"I'm sorry, but Mr. Nash isn't available right now," the secretary reported.

"I see. Will he be in later today?"

"I'm afraid not. He's out of the country."

Out of the country? "Are you sure?"

"Yes, ma'am," the secretary drawled. "Would y'all like me to transfer your call to Mr. Hartwick or Mr. Brennigan?"

"No. Thank you," she mumbled, then hung up the phone.

She sank weakly into a chair and tried to shake her head clear. She had known Bobby Lee for such a long time. She'd thought she could depend on him. Throughout the years of their relationship, he had never once done anything underhanded.

Something about diamonds seemed to bring out the beast in a person, she supposed.

They're only stones, she told herself. She had her life, her health, and Jack Slater's love. So what if Bobby Lee had swindled her? What difference did it make?

Not much. Yet her worry gnawed at her all day. The diamonds didn't matter, but her stupidity in trusting Bobby Lee did.

When Jack called her that evening, he heard the tremor in her voice. "Mandy, what's wrong?"

"Nothing," she told him, then cringed. She didn't like lying to him.

Evidently Jack sensed she was keeping something from him. "Mandy?"

"It's nothing, really." *Be honest,* she chided herself. *Losing the diamonds is nothing. Losing Jack because you lied to him would be the worst thing in the world.* "I'm sorry, Jack, it's just . . . the diamonds . . . I'm a fool."

"What about the diamonds?" His tone was altered, less cajoling, more wary. "Mandy, has anyone gone after you? Has that jackass Stevenson shown his godforsaken face in Kentucky? So help me, if he's come within a hundred miles of you, I swear I'll—"

"No, Jack. No. It's not him."

Jack sounded even more wary when he said, "Who is it?"

"Well, it's ... Bobby Lee."

A long, tense silence ensued before Jack spoke. "What about Bobby Lee?"

"He has the diamonds."

"What the hell are you talking about?"

"I had to hide them somewhere. It wasn't safe to have them in Harrow—not just for me, but for my brother. I had to get them out of town."

She waited for him to concur, but he said nothing.

"And I couldn't bring them to New York with me. I've heard tell New York is full of crime, muggers and that sort of thing—"

"Oh, yes, indeed. Unlike peaceful Harrow, Kentucky, where they have so little crime the police department justifies its existence by locking innocent people in jail. Sure, crime-free Harrow, where everyone owns a gun and your grandfather was a moonshiner."

"Jack, please—"

"So you gave them to Bobby Lee?" he continued, ignoring her interruption. "Your old boyfriend?"

His rage splashed against her like gasoline on smoldering embers, making them flare into small, painful bursts of flame. She was so angry with herself, she couldn't bear to be angry with Jack, too, or to have him angry with her.

But if she was burning from small bursts of flame, he was a veritable thermonuclear explosion. "Bobby

Lee? Damn it, Mandy, why not *me?* Why didn't you come to *me* with this?''

"Before I went to New York, the last time I saw you was when you walked out of my life. Remember?'' She didn't give him a chance to answer this time. "As far as I knew, you'd left me for good. I went to New York to get your doll for you, because I felt I owed it to you. I had no intention of…well, of anything else.''

"What are you saying? Making love with me was unintentional?''

Why was he twisting around everything she said? "I thought you didn't love me, Jack. I thought you didn't want me. I thought all you wanted was the doll, and I reckoned there was no way you could get it without me.''

"So you turned to your old boyfriend for help. The love of your life, ol' Bobby Lee Nash.''

"Because he's a lawyer and all—''

"Because you trusted him more than you trusted me.''

She took a deep breath and prayed for calm. She had thought Jack would be sympathetic. Instead he was acting more like a lawyer than Bobby Lee ever had. A prosecuting attorney.

"I thought I could trust him,'' she said wearily. "I made a mistake. It's not the first time, and I daresay it won't be the last.''

"You made a mistake.'' Jack's voice dripped with bitter sarcasm. "So what happened?''

"He seems to have skipped town. His secretary told me he's out of the country."

Jack cursed. Something in the single vile syllable caused her back to stiffen. She had assured herself that losing her diamonds was irrelevant as long as she had Jack's love. She had also assured herself that she had Jack's love.

Obviously she didn't.

"Well, all right, then," she muttered, not bothering to stifle her hostility. "I made a mistake. I'm a bad judge of character." *Especially when it comes to men,* she added silently. "I'm just an ol' hillbilly fool."

"Mandy—"

"I'm just a hayseed hick from a Kentucky holler." Her words came faster, surer, sputtering out of her like bullets out of a machine gun. "A moonshiner's granddaughter. Poor white trash. So I reckon you won't be having any need of me anymore—"

"Mandy, get real," he interrupted. "This isn't about being a hayseed from a Kentucky holler. This is about your conspiring with your old boyfriend behind my back—"

"Conspiring? For heaven's sake! Bobby Lee doesn't have anything to do with us."

"He has everything to do with us. You had a dilemma and you turned to him. The man you lived with for two years. The man you almost married."

"He's my friend."

"I'm sure he is. In your next lifetime, Mandy, I suggest you choose your friends more carefully."

"Jack—"

"You should have trusted *me.*"

"I didn't have you!"

"Yeah." His tone was as subdued as hers was enraged. "I guess you didn't. Look, I've got to go. Maybe your old lover will turn up and you'll live happily ever after. I wish you all the luck in the world."

She heard a click, and then the line went dead.

Chapter Thirteen

He considered breaking something. But breaking things was his father's way of expressing anger, and Jack had spent the better part of his life trying to mature into the kind of man his father had never been.

So he didn't break anything. He just cursed.

A lot.

And pounded the dining room table a few times for good measure.

How could she have gone to Bobby Lee with this?

They were friends, she'd said. Sure. Jack did his best to remain on friendly terms with former girlfriends—but he wouldn't entrust them with millions of dollars of assets that could be easily transported out of the country.

That Bobby Lee wasn't trustworthy meant little to Jack. That Mandy had lost her diamonds meant little to Jack.

What he cared about was her trust. What he cared about was that when she'd needed someone she'd turned to Bobby Lee.

Damn. Jack was in love with her. Obviously he was as bad a judge of character as she was, at least when it came to matters of the heart.

On the other hand... His rage gradually sorted itself out into hurt and suspicion. Suspicion that her judgment might be just fine.

For all Jack knew, Mandy had been lying to him all along. Maybe she'd stuck with Jack just long enough to make certain the various and sundry villains in this escapade could never come back after her. Now that she was safe from them, she could return to the arms of her beloved Southern beau.

Maybe Bobby Lee hadn't bolted with the gems—or maybe he had, along with Mandy. Maybe they were on that tropical island Jack had imagined one damp, dreary afternoon while he'd been locked up in Harrow's police department holding cell with nothing better to think about.

Maybe the whole thing had been an incredibly convoluted setup. It might as well have been, given the way Jack felt: like a first-class, A-1 chump.

Okay. It was done. History. He'd simply have to get over her.

Yet when he crawled into bed later that night, the two large glasses of whiskey he'd consumed did nothing to numb him. He lay alone in the dark, silent room, recalling her scent, the wild cascade of her hair, the silky feel of her skin, the weight of her breasts filling his hands. Groaning, he recalled the pressure of her lips on his, the sweet taste of her, the tightness of her body drawing him in, throbbing around him, and her low, sultry voice moaning in blissful surrender....

It's over, he reminded himself. The time he'd spent with her—and the passion he'd felt for her—had been nothing more than a detour from reality. Everything had happened too fast; everything had seemed too intense. He'd been bewitched by Mandy's beauty, her talent and her courage. Bewitched wasn't the same thing as being in love.

He would be smart to remember that.

His miserable, restless night showed plainly on his face the next morning. His eyes were bloodshot and circled in shadow, his mouth locked into a scowl, his mood ominous. It was going to be a fun day, he could tell.

He growled his surly way through a couple of morning appointments. When his secretary asked if he was feeling well, he warned her to leave him a wide berth. She wisely backed out of his office, promising to hold his calls to a minimum.

The office grew quiet. He heard whispers outside his door but ignored them. He spent most of the afternoon staring at a software-setup contract for a sporting-goods chain on Long Island. Not a single line of print registered on him.

Hell, it took weeks to get over the flu. It was going to take longer than that to get over Mandy Harlon. He might as well get used to feeling lousy.

Sometime late in the afternoon he heard his secretary's voice through his closed door. "No, I'm sorry but he isn't seeing anyone today."

"He'll see me," came a gravelly voice Jack recognized at once. The door swung open.

"Moe," Jack grunted, slumping in his chair and swiveling around to gaze out the window.

"I know, I know. You're not seeing anyone," said Moe as he shut the door behind him and sauntered across the room to a plush leather chair in front of Jack's desk. "It's obvious you're not seeing anyone. You were supposed to be seeing me at Flannagan's for lunch today."

Jack groaned. He'd forgotten all about their weekly lunch, and his secretary had dutifully not bothered to remind him. "Sorry."

"Forgive me, Jack, but you look like hell."

"You're forgiven."

"So." Moe rapped his misshapen knuckles against the edge of Jack's desk, beating a quiet tattoo. "Have you been to the doctor?"

"I'm not sick," he said, swiveling back to face Moe. "I had a rough night, that's all."

Moe held up a hand. "Spare me the details—I don't want to know." A smile of comprehension tickled his lips. "Mandy's in town? Why didn't you say so? I'd love to see her. Maybe I could make a party. Betsy Rudolph adores her, you know."

"Betsy Rudolph adores everybody."

"And you adore nobody," Moe surmised in reaction to Jack's dour mood. "So, Mandy's in town?"

"No." Jack leaned far enough back in his chair that he could view the ceiling. "I don't know where she is. Her boyfriend's run off with her diamonds, though."

"Her boyfriend?" Moe scowled. "I thought you were her boyfriend."

"Apparently I'm not." Jack sighed. "I don't want to talk about it, Moe."

"Fine. We won't talk about it." Moe obediently embarked on a monologue about the wretched round of handball he'd played at the club that afternoon, about Nadine's niece's wedding, about how the ceramic tiles in the third-floor bathroom needed new grouting.

"All right," Moe finally said when he realized he couldn't guilt Jack into dinner, "I'll see you another time." Moe stood and leaned forward, planting his hands on the blotter and bearing down on Jack. "Take care of yourself."

"Of course I'll take care of myself," Jack promised impatiently. At his age, he resented Moe treating him like a child.

"What do you want, Jack? You want to lose her? You want her never again in your life? Fine. If that's what you want."

Jack's resentment evolved into sorrow. He swallowed his reflexive retort. It wasn't Moe's fault that Mandy had turned out to be a duplicitous witch.

"What I want," he said quietly, "is a woman who comes to me when she's got a problem."

"Like Mandy came to you in New York."

"She went to you, Moe, not me. She went to her old fiancé and to you. She doesn't want me."

"Fine. She doesn't want you. So don't waste your energy trying to get her back."

"That's right."

"Take care of yourself." Moe gave Jack's cheek a pat, a gentle, affectionate tap that nonetheless reminded Jack of the sort of slap one might use to shock a person out of a stupor. He glowered at Moe as the older man turned and strode to the door. "I'll be around if you want to talk," Moe said before he vanished from the office.

Jack left for home soon afterward. He wasn't getting any work done anyway. Maybe tomorrow, after a good night's sleep, he'd be able to concentrate.

He didn't have a good night's sleep, though. That night, memories of Mandy were interspersed with scraps of Moe's visit—the words, the paternal pat on the cheek, the advice. *Don't waste your energy trying to get her back....*

Damn Moe. Maybe it wasn't his fault that Mandy had deceived Jack, but it *was* Moe's fault that Jack had met Mandy in the first place. Moe's, and that blasted doll's fault. Who ever heard of a doll curing arthritis?

Eventually Jack did drift off, only to oversleep. He flinched awake with a start, discovered it was nearly nine-thirty, and stumbled out of bed. From the other end of the apartment he heard a clamor.

Trudging down the hall, he realized what had roused him was the strident buzz of his intercom near the front door. He lifted the receiver, rubbing the sleep from his burning eyes. "Yeah?" he growled into the mouthpiece.

"There's an express-mail delivery here for you, Mr. Slater," the doorman informed him. "Do you want me to sign for it or send the postman upstairs?"

"Send him up."

He heated a cup of coffee for himself, then returned to the entry to answer the doorbell. A postal carrier handed him a parcel and asked for his signature. Jack didn't dare to look at the return address until he was alone again.

Harrow, Kentucky.

He carried the box into the kitchen and took a long, scalding swig of coffee. It sharpened his mind enough to make him consider telephoning the office and letting his secretary know he was running late. Yet the box beckoned him. He had to open it first. Once he did, he would know what to do with the rest of his morning—maybe the rest of his life.

With a steak knife he sliced the tape. Then, pulling back the flaps, he dug through crumpled wads of newspaper and lifted out . . . the Moe doll.

Touching it sent a shock through his system, a jolt of memory, of heat and need and anger. He dropped the doll as if it had singed his fingertips.

Examining it from a distance, he would have guessed she'd made an entirely new doll, but when he moved closer, he saw evidence of restoration: the tiny hand stitches along what used to be a tear, the lighter patches of hair.

The way the doll had landed when Jack dropped it, it appeared to be seated on the table, leaning back against the side of the shipping carton. It gazed up at him as if to say, in Moe's distinctive scratchy New York voice, "So? Take care of yourself."

Hesitantly Jack picked up the doll again. He considered the weight of the pebbles inside it, the hard chips giving it form.

He knew it was filled with rose-quartz crystal. Not because Mandy mishandled the diamonds, not because he'd told her not to use them, but because...

Because when he held the doll in his hands, he felt better. His mind cleared. His mood brightened. He didn't believe any of that New Age silliness about crystals, rose quartz or otherwise, but...

If the doll could make his wish come true, he'd have Mandy back.

And suddenly, for some reason, he found himself believing.

HE DELIBERATELY chose a different car-rental agency at the airport in Huntington, West Virginia, just in case the agency he'd used last time had him entered in their computer as a maniac who drove cars off cliffs. Tossing his bag into the back seat, he headed out onto the highway, hoping that when he got to Harrow he would find Mandy there.

He had telephoned her twice but she hadn't answered. "Go anyway," Moe had urged him when he'd brought Moe his doll. "What have you got to lose?"

"The airfare, for starters."

"So? It's just money. What else have you got to lose? A day or two?"

"My pride. My sanity."

"There's such a thing as too much sanity, Jack. And too much pride. Go. Worse comes to worst, you'll come back and know you tried."

Jack had every intention of trying. If Mandy wasn't home, he'd track down Jessie, or go after Bobby Lee Nash.

He wasn't sure whether this trip would end happily. But, as Moe had said, Jack wouldn't be able to live with himself if he didn't try.

The last time he was in the eastern Kentucky border country, it had been a dismal, rainy period. Now, with May just days away, the Appalachian sky was a vivid blue, the air dry, the trees dense with rich green foliage. Crab apple trees were lacy with blossoms; daisies and wild roses splashed their pastel hues along the sides of the winding asphalt. Instead of seeming crazy to him this time, the mountain roads seemed beautiful and not the least bit difficult to navigate.

He refused to take that as a positive omen.

He reached Harrow in under an hour. Cruising along Main Street, he spotted Bill McIntyre's mud-spattered Bronco parked across the street from the Sunnyside Café. He knew this place; he almost felt at home here.

Don't get your hopes up, he cautioned himself. He could be setting himself up for a fall far worse than any plunge into a roadside ravine. When he confronted Mandy, she might toss her lustrous mane of blazing curls and drawl, "I changed my mind, Jack. I reckon I want to tie my fate to a lawyer with a pure Southern bloodline. You-all have a good life now."

Then again, she might not even be in the country.

He left the tiny downtown district for the twisting, climbing road out into the hills. After a while, the rustic mailbox with Harlon painted on its side loomed into view around a bend in the road.

He braked the car and took stock. What optimism he'd had just minutes ago began to wane. He didn't want her slamming her door on him. He didn't think he could stand it.

Then he thought about the doll, the way it had felt in his hands, the way its promise had infused him. He guided his foot back to the gas pedal and drove up onto her driveway.

Climbing out of the car, he heard it. Jazz. Something low and mournful, a solo saxophone wailing through an open window and across the overgrown front yard. The tune was depressing, but Jack took heart in the soulful sound.

Mandy was home. There was hope.

He marched to the front porch and tugged the door. To his surprise, it was locked.

"Mandy!" he shouted through the music. "Open up! It's—"

"Jack!" She finished the sentence, standing in the suddenly open door and gaping at him.

Poignant music swirled around them like gossamer threads, drawing them together. If she'd stopped him, if she'd resisted in any way, he would have backed off. But as his arms came around her waist she looped hers around his neck and pulled his face down to hers, kissing him as if her life depended on it.

Before he could get totally lost in the kiss she broke from him, clapping her hand to her mouth and taking a step backward. He heard his breath, shallow and rasping. He felt the strain in his body, and the dash of ice in his soul as he read confusion in her eyes. "What?" he asked.

Abashed, she averted her gaze. "I shouldn't have thrown myself at you like that. It's just, I've missed you, and..."

He began to feel a hell of a lot better. "And what?"

"And the least I could do is find out what you came for. Last time it was the doll."

He ran his gaze down her lush body to her beautiful bare toes and back up again to her face. She had apparently tied her hair back with a ribbon some time ago, and her face was framed by untamable waves that had leaked out of the ponytail. Her cheeks were pink, her eyes wide and glistening.

A living doll, he thought—only she was so much more. "I came for you," he said, then kissed her again.

He tried to exercise restraint, but it was next to impossible. How could he restrain himself when he had Mandy in his arms, her breasts swelling against his chest, her clean, womanly fragrance filling his nostrils? How could he restrain himself when she was weaving her fingers into the hair at his temples and nibbling his lower lip with her teeth and tongue?

How long had it been since he'd held her? Less than a week. It felt like an eternity.

"Let me come in," he demanded.

"Yes," she said breathlessly, backing into the front room. "Yes. Come in."

Somehow they managed to move inside the doorway. It wasn't easy with their arms locked around each other and their lips continuing to nip and tease and fuse. His blood pulsed hot and urgent through his veins, and he dropped his hands to her bottom and hauled her against him. He needed her, needed her as he'd never needed anything before.

"I missed you so much," he whispered, yanking her blouse free from her jeans and sliding one hand up her back, savoring the satin warmth of her skin. He entertained a moment's curiosity about what amazing lingerie she might be wearing—until he reached the nape of her neck and realized she wasn't wearing anything at all under her blouse. Skimming forward, he caught one full, firm breast in his hand and groaned.

"You never even called me," she argued when her ragged breath allowed her the voice to speak.

He circled her budding nipple with his fingertips and she gasped. "I thought you'd run off with Bobby Lee," he said, bringing his other hand forward and groping for her fly. "I thought you and he had run off together."

In spite of her obvious arousal, she erupted in laughter. "Run off with a scalawag like him? Why in God's name would you think such a thing?"

As much as he wanted her, he forced himself to withdraw. His hands ached with emptiness, and his body just ached. But they had to talk first. They had to work this out.

He took a step back and let out a long, steadying breath. "You used to love him," he said.

Her smile faded. A flourish of minor-key notes spilled out of the sound system in the kitchen. "I didn't know what love was till I met you, Jack. If you can't believe that—"

He pulled her into his arms and buried his lips in the thick, silky hair. "I do believe you. And I want to believe that whenever you need help, I'm the guy you'll come to. Whenever you're in trouble, I'm the guy who'll save you. Call me selfish, but I don't want to share you with your old boyfriend."

"He's not my boyfriend, Jack. He hasn't been for years."

"Yeah, well..." Jack dug his hands into his pockets and nudged a crack in the linoleum floor with his toe. "Well, I'm jealous, all right?"

"Even when you have no reason to be?"

He offered a crooked smile. "I need reassurance."

She gazed up at him. Her expression was earnest, her eyes clear and constant as she peered into his face. "I love you, Jack. I've spent a lot of time this past week wishing it weren't so, but it is. I'm doomed. I love you."

"We're both doomed," he murmured, extending his arms to her.

She bravely, eagerly, melted into his embrace. As his mouth crushed down on hers, he heard a distant sound, not jazz but something jangling.

Her telephone.

"Oh, Lord," she sighed. "It must be Iris again. I've spent more time at her house than my own lately. Seems she and Jessie are reconciling. As long as one of them can't talk, they get along real well."

"There's more than one way to communicate," Jack pointed out, thinking about the specific way he wanted to communicate with Mandy as soon as she was done on the phone.

He followed her into the kitchen, where she lifted the receiver. "Hello?" She listened for a moment, her face darkening, her brow dipping in a frown. "Where in tarnation...? You what?"

Jack leaned against the doorframe, refamiliarizing himself with her busy kitchen, her workbench, her stereo speakers and appliances. He didn't mean to eavesdrop on her, but he couldn't stop staring at her, admiring her, lusting after her, imagining the joy of sharing a doom with her.

"Well, I reckon," she said into the phone. "It's a mite odd, Bobby Lee, but..."

Bobby Lee? Jack stood straighter.

"No, that's all right, I understand. No apology necessary. Just stick it in the mail.... Really, Bobby, I'm grateful."

Grateful for what?

She bade Bobby Lee goodbye, hung up, and turned to Jack. "That ol' fool," she said.

"What about him?"

"He just got back from a vacation trip to Cancun."

"Terrific."

"He found the key."

"What key?"

"To the safe-deposit box where he put my diamonds. Oh, Jack—I'm so relieved. I felt like such an idiot, trusting him. He's always been a friend to me—and I don't say that to make you jealous, Jack, but even though Bobby Lee and I weren't right for each other, he was a decent fellow."

"Uh-huh." Jack blew off his momentary jealousy. Mandy had said she was doomed to love him. He could be generous in victory. "So he put your diamonds in a safe-deposit box?"

"In a big bank in Atlanta. He acted as my legal representative, so the box is in my name. I can go there and get the diamonds whenever I want, once I have the key. He'd meant to send it to me before he left for Mexico, but he was kind of in a tizzy and he forgot to stick it in the mail. It's been sitting on his dresser all this time."

"I see."

"Anyway, he said he'd send it out in tomorrow's post. He also said his nose was peeling and I really ought to go to Cancun sometime. He said it's awful lovely."

"Well, assuming he's telling the truth about your diamonds, you can probably afford to go anywhere you want."

A sly smile curved her lips. The seductive light in her stunning blue eyes tugged at his nerves, making his muscles clench and his breath catch. "Let's go to my bedroom," she drawled in that marvelous sultry voice of hers. "That's exactly where I want to go."

"What a coincidence," Jack whispered, gathering her into his arms once more. "That's exactly where I want to go, too."

Epilogue

They didn't go to Cancun.

They went, instead, to an island two hours by boat from Tahiti. It wasn't quite small enough for them to have the entire island to themselves, but Jack supposed there was something to be said for a well-staffed hotel. The food was superb. The concierge was courteous. The sheets and towels were changed every day, which Jack greatly appreciated, considering how much time he and Mandy spent in bed and luxuriating together in the jacuzzi.

He would never have guessed that doom could be this much fun.

He was on the beach now, stretched out on the pearl white sand in the shade of a cluster of palm trees. Thirty feet south of his toes, the beach met a turquoise ocean. Six inches west of his left hand stood a frosty glass filled with pineapple juice and rum. Six inches east of his right lay the mystery novel he hadn't bothered to open since they'd arrived a week ago.

A shadow moving along the sand captured his attention. He propped himself up on his elbows and gazed at Mandy, who walked in graceful sure-footed strides across the pliant sand. Her skin glowed with a delicate honey-gold undertone, and the bright midafternoon sunlight burnished her hair, igniting the profuse red waves.

Grinning, Mandy dropped her tote bag on the straw mat next to Jack's towel and sat beside him. "Guess what?"

"What?"

"You've got mail."

"I most certainly do," he punned playfully, pulling her down on top of him. He nudged the narrow straps of her swimsuit top down her shoulders and leaned to press his lips to the hollow between her breasts.

With feigned indignation Mandy slapped his hands away and straightened out her swimsuit. "Get your 'male' under control, Jack. I meant m-a-i-l. A letter."

"A letter?" No one was supposed to know where he and Mandy were. No one except Moe.

"From Moe," she confirmed, pulling the cream-colored envelope out of her tote and handing it to Jack.

A frisson of worry shot through him. Why would Moe write to him? He and Mandy were due back in New York next week, after a brief layover in Phoenix to visit her parents. Surely anything Moe had to say to them could wait until then—unless it was an emergency.

He tore open the envelope, pulled out the letter and read aloud.

"'Dear Jack and Mandy. Just a line to let you know Mandy's things arrived at my house safe and sound.'" Jack rolled his eyes. To Moe, who had lived at the same address for forty years, dealing with a moving company qualified as an emergency, even if the move went smoothly. "'Everything was left stacked in the cellar, where it will remain out of the way until you find a house. At the last minute, her brother and sister-in-law told me they were going to drive up her stereo system and her CD collection personally. I insisted they stay here at the house a few days. They are a delightful couple, although they do have a habit of talking at the same time and disagreeing loudly.'"

"I warned Jessie," Mandy said, clicking her tongue. "I told him if he and Iris were going to get married again, one or the other of them ought to have their jaw wired shut during waking hours."

"Jessie's supposed to talk a lot, isn't he? It's part of his therapy, building up his jaw muscles." Jack shook the notepaper smooth and resumed reading. "'So,'" the letter went on, "'I hope you are having a good time, and I remind you that it is never too soon to make me a grandpa.'"

"He's terrible," Jack groaned.

"He's wonderful," Mandy countered.

Jack didn't argue. "'Love, Moe,'" he read. "'P.S. You will note that my handwriting has improved. My fingers have developed even more flexibility over the past few weeks. The doll has lived up to its promise.'"

Still laughing, Mandy took the letter from Jack and slipped it back into the envelope. "He ought to get a second opinion on that. I reckon his doctor won't agree."

"Who cares what his doctor thinks? If Moe says his hands feel better, that's what counts."

"It's probably all in his head. What's that called, the placebo effect? He thinks it'll make him better, so it does."

Ordinarily Jack would have agreed. But when it came to Mandy's dolls with their rose-quartz crystal stuffing, he believed every bit as much as Moe did. "It's all in my head, too," he said. "That doll you made for him is capable of working magic."

"That doll, plus a bottle of aspirin."

"Don't be a cynic," Jack scolded. "You made the doll. You charged me a hundred fifty bucks for it."

"You want your money back?"

"Why should I want my money back? It works."

"Maybe Moe's hands feel better because the weather's warmer."

"Or because the stars are in alignment," Jack teased. "Or because he's happy for us. Or because—" he drew her down onto his towel and held her close "—you made the doll. Don't tell me it doesn't work. It brought us together, right?"

"Well, yes, but—"

"And doesn't that prove the thing's got magical powers?"

"It only proves," she countered, "that I'm a talented doll maker and you're a stubborn, impatient scoundrel who couldn't wait an extra minute for me to finish the damned thing and ship it to New York properly."

"An extra minute? I waited four months!"

"How long are we going to be having this argument?" Mandy asked, her eyes growing luminous and her mouth softening into an alluring smile.

Jack smiled, as well. "At least a thousand years," he vowed, pulling her down for a kiss. He closed his eyes to savor the feel of her, the warm, luscious desire her lips awakened deep inside him.

He shifted onto his side. His swim trunks didn't hide much, and even though no one was close enough to see, he thought his physical state called for discretion.

The fronds of the palm trees shifted in a citrus-scented breeze, allowing narrow stripes of sunshine to flutter over his body and Mandy's. The light caused her ring to glint.

He clasped her hand in his and brushed her fingertips with his lips. The diamonds looked surprisingly right on her, a neat, evenly matched band of brilliant stones set in elegant white gold, circling her left ring finger. It wasn't the sort of ring one would expect to find on a backwoods hick.

Then again, Mandy was no ordinary backwoods hick. And this was no ordinary wedding band. Nestled amid the diamonds was a single polished chip of rose-quartz crystal. It was easy to overlook, easy to ignore. But Jack and Mandy knew it was there.

The diamonds gave the ring its value, but the rose-quartz crystal gave it its magic. And as long as Mandy had that ring on her finger and her hand in his, Jack knew everything there was to know about wishes coming true.

American Romance invites you to celebrate a decade of success....

It's a year of celebration for American Romance, as we commemorate a milestone achievement—10 years of bringing you the kinds of romance novels you want to read, by the authors you've come to love.

And we're not stopping now! In the months ahead, we'll be bringing you more of the adventures of a lifetime...and some superspecial anniversary surprises.

We've got lots in store, so mark your calendars to join us, beginning in August, for all the fun of our 10th Anniversary year....

AMERICAN ROMANCE
We'll rouse your lust for adventure!

THREE UNFORGETTABLE HEROINES
THREE AWARD-WINNING AUTHORS

Untamed

MAVERICK HEARTS

A unique collection of historical short stories that capture the spirit of America's last frontier.

HEATHER GRAHAM POZZESSERE—over 10 million copies of her books in print worldwide
Lonesome Rider—The story of an Eastern widow and the renegade half-breed who becomes her protector.

PATRICIA POTTER—an author whose books are consistently Waldenbooks bestsellers
Against the Wind—Two people, battered by heartache, prove that love can heal all.

JOAN JOHNSTON—award-winning Western historical author with 17 books to her credit
One Simple Wish—A woman with a past discovers that dreams really do come true.

Join us for an exciting journey West with
UNTAMED
Available in July, wherever Harlequin books are sold.

Fifty red-blooded, white-hot, true-blue hunks from every
State in the Union!

Beginning in May, look for MEN MADE IN AMERICA!
Written by some of our most popular authors, these
stories feature fifty of the strongest, sexiest men, each
from a different state in the union!

Two titles available every other month at your favorite
retail outlet.

In July, look for:

CALL IT DESTINY by Jayne Ann Krentz (Arizona)
ANOTHER KIND OF LOVE by Mary Lynn Baxter
(Arkansas)

In September, look for:

DECEPTIONS by Annette Broadrick (California)
STORMWALKER by Dallas Schulze (Colorado)

You won't be able to resist MEN MADE IN AMERICA!

HARLEQUIN®

AMERICAN ◆ ROMANCE®

Four new stars shine a silvery light on American Romance's 10th Anniversary!

Catch a...

Rising Star

Over the past decade, American Romance has launched over 40 first-time authors—and made stars of a dozen more. And in August a new constellation appears—the stars of tomorrow—four authors brand-new to American Romance:

#497 **AT HER CAPTAIN'S COMMAND**
        by Patricia Chandler
#498 **DATE WITH AN OUTLAW** by Lynn Lockhart
#499 **ONE FOOT IN HEAVEN** by Laraine McDaniel
#500 **WILD CARD WEDDING** by Jule McBride

In August 1993 catch the excitement—
Catch a ''Rising Star''!